Sculpture Sabotage

Bang! A clang rang out, making Nancy jump about a foot in the air.

She didn't waste a second. She raced past the art building, with Bess right behind her. The shadowy shapes of the sculpture garden came into sight in the distance.

"It's hard to tell what's a sculpture," Nancy said, "and what's a tree or a—"

"There!" Bess cried, pointing. "Next to Rhoda's new sculpture."

Nancy's eyes flew to the spot where they had installed the sculpture that afternoon. Sure enough, right next to the sculpture was the jet black silhouette of a person.

Nancy gasped as the person raised something high in the air. "A sledgehammer!" she said, then shouted, "Stop!"

Even as she screamed the word, Nancy saw the sledgehammer being swung down. It smashed into the sculpture with a splintering crack that chilled her.

Nancy Drew
Mystery Stories

Available from Simon & Schuster

NANCY DREW® 166

THE CASE OF THE CREATIVE CRIME

CAROLYN KEENE

Aladdin Paperbacks
New York   London   Toronto   Sydney   Singapore

First Aladdin Paperbacks edition May 2002

Copyright © 2002 Simon & Schuster, Inc.

ALADDIN PAPERBACKS
An imprint of Simon & Schuster
Children's Publishing Division
1230 Avenue of the Americas
New York, NY 10020

Printed in the United States of America

10 9 8 7 6 5 4 3 2 1

NANCY DREW and NANCY DREW MYSTERY STORIES are registered trademarks of Simon & Schuster, Inc.

ISBN 0-7434-3748-9

Library of Congress Control Number 2001096928

Contents

1

Man of the Year

"So, how does it feel to be the daughter of the River Heights Man of the Year?" Bess Marvin turned in the passenger seat of Nancy Drew's blue Mustang convertible and grinned at her friend. She held up a copy of the *River Heights News*, letting the edges flap in the warm summer breeze. "He's right on the front page and everything!"

Nancy took her eyes away from the road long enough to glance at the grainy photograph of her dad, who smiled out from the newspaper page. Just above the photo, the headline read, "Carson Drew Honored for Civic Achievements." Every time she read the words, Nancy thought she would burst with pride.

"Isn't it great?" she said. "Dad says he's been in

1

shock since the mayor called to tell him about the award yesterday. I guess he never realized how much he's done for the town over the years."

"Are you kidding? The list of good stuff he helped make happen in River Heights is about a mile long!" Bess skimmed the article. "The drive to rebuild the waterfront, community workfare programs, saving the old railway station from being demolished, helping start a local arts colony . . ." Her voice trailed off into a laugh. "Is there any good deed your dad *hasn't* done?"

"There must be a few old ladies he hasn't helped across the street yet," Nancy said.

Bess propped her sunglasses on top of her head, anchoring her blond hair back from her face. "He'll have to get to work on that—after he takes us out to lunch, that is," she said.

The dinner honoring Nancy's father wouldn't take place until Saturday, four days away. But Carson had insisted on celebrating the good news right away by taking Nancy and Bess to lunch. He would have invited Bess's cousin George, too, because Bess and George had been Nancy's best friends since they were little kids, but George was away on a two-week bike trip.

"Lunch at Emilio's." Bess gave a dreamy sigh as Nancy pulled into the parking lot next to the building in which Carson's law office was located. "Forget about the rest of your dad's accomplishments. Treating us to lunch at the best Italian restaurant in River Heights is enough to make him Man of the Year in my book. My mouth is watering already."

"Mine, too." Nancy parked her car in an empty spot, then got out and smoothed the silky fabric of the sleeveless dress she wore. The deep blue dress matched the color of her eyes perfectly and made her reddish blond hair stand out.

"Ugh!" Nancy squinted as a blast of hot, dusty air blew across the parking lot from a construction site just down the street. A steady drone came from the hulking cranes and bulldozers that were visible through an opening in the wooden barrier surrounding the site. "Swallowing dust and diesel fumes wasn't exactly the appetizer I had in mind."

"That's for sure," Bess said. She tucked her newspaper into her shoulder bag, then brushed off some grit from the white wraparound blouse she wore with a flowered skirt. "Let's get out of here before we turn into a couple of dust balls."

They hurried out of the parking lot and into the office building. The heat and dust and noise disappeared the moment they stepped into the lobby. Nancy enjoyed the cool air-conditioning as she and Bess rode the elevator up to her father's office.

"Hear that?" Bess stepped into the hallway and cupped a hand to her ear. Laughter rang out into the hallway from Carson's office. "It sounds as if your dad's already celebrating."

Nancy pushed open the door to the office suite and stepped inside. The desk where Carson's legal secretary, Ms. Hanson, usually sat was empty. She was probably out to lunch, Nancy thought. Through an open door beyond the secretary's desk, Nancy saw her dad sitting at his desk in his suit and tie. Carson's brown hair was laced with gray at the temples. His dark eyes gleamed as he laughed and talked with someone Nancy couldn't see.

"Is it twelve-thirty already?" Carson asked when he saw Nancy. He got up to give her and Bess hugs, then ushered them into his office. "Come on in, girls. There's someone here I'd like you to meet."

The woman sitting across from Carson looked to be in her early thirties. She had dark brown skin, shoulder-length braids, intelligent amber eyes, and a rich laugh that made Nancy like her right away.

"I'm Rhoda Benton," the woman said, introducing herself. As she stood up to shake hands with Nancy and Bess, Nancy saw that she was impressively tall. She wore a necklace of turquoise beads over a tunic that flowed loosely over her pants. A bright woven shoulder bag lay on the floor beside her chair.

"Carson tells me you've got lunch plans, but I couldn't resist stopping by to congratulate the man who helped me turn my life around." Rhoda shook

4

her head slowly back and forth. "Let me tell you, before I entered the workfare program Carson helped set up, I was in pretty sorry shape."

"What do you mean?" Bess asked.

"Rhoda has always been talented," Carson said, "and smart. But it took her awhile to find direction in her life."

"That's a polite way of saying I was a troubled teenager who was constantly up to no good," Rhoda said. "I hung out with a pretty rough crowd, cut school. . . . Eventually I was arrested for breaking into a warehouse."

"Wow," Nancy said. Rhoda seemed so happy and . . . decent. It was hard to imagine her breaking the law.

"Is that how you got into the workfare program?" Bess asked. She pointed to the folded-up newspaper that stuck out of her shoulder bag. "According to the article about Mr. Drew in the *News,* that was a program for rehabilitating first-time offenders."

"That's right," Carson told her. "I worked with a few other lawyers and some politicians to find an alternative to jail for people convicted of minor crimes—if they didn't have previous criminal records, that is."

Rhoda nodded. "Instead of going to jail, I received counseling and did community service," she said. "Luckily for me, my service was working in a woodworking shop. This might sound funny, but it was the first time I ever did something I cared about. I loved working with the tools and seeing how I could make a couple of pieces of wood turn into a beautiful shelf or cabinet or table. It changed my life."

"After completing the workfare program, Rhoda was accepted to art school," Carson said. "Twelve years later here she is, a successful sculptor who's opening an arts colony in River Heights."

"The place that's opening up on the old Pennington estate north of town?" Bess asked. Pulling the folded newspaper from her shoulder bag, she said, "There's something about it in today's paper. What's the arts colony called again?"

"River Arts," Carson said. When Bess unfolded the paper, he pointed to a photograph of Rhoda and a group of teenagers standing around a cubelike sculpture in front of some rosebushes. The caption read: "At River Arts, students and teachers take time to smell the roses."

"It looks like a beautiful place," Nancy said.

"It is. We're lucky Carson was able to convince the owner to let River Arts lease the estate and convert it to an arts colony," Rhoda said. She shook her head in amazement. "I don't know how you did it, Carson. Marianna Pennington is one stubborn old lady."

Nancy's father laughed. "Stubborn, yes. But not unreasonable. Marianna couldn't afford to keep up that huge house anymore, not to mention all the old outbuildings and grounds," Carson said. "But she didn't want to move or sell the place, either. Once she learned that River Arts would maintain the buildings and she could go on living in a wing of the house, Mrs. Pennington was sold on the plan to lease the place to River Arts."

"I guess Marianna realized that sharing her estate with a bunch of crazy artists wouldn't be nearly as bad as losing it altogether," Rhoda said.

She slung the straps of her bag over her shoulder and walked with Carson, Nancy, and Bess to the elevator. As they all got into the elevator car, Nancy tried to recall what her father had told her about the new arts colony. "River Arts is for college students, isn't it, Ms. Benton?" she asked.

"Please, call me Rhoda. Everyone does," Rhoda said. "And yes, River Arts *is* for college kids. Students sign up for classes and individual work sessions with established painters, sculptors, dancers, and performance artists. It's a chance for kids to focus on their art and to work with some of the best professionals in their field."

"That sounds great," Bess said, her eyes sparkling.

"It is," said Rhoda. "We're starting with a summer program, but students can take a semester away from their college during the school year, too. Our first group of students arrived just a few days ago. We've been busy getting studios and work routines

7

set up. Everyone is really excited." Rhoda smiled to herself before going on. "Especially me. I guess River Arts is my way of giving kids the opportunities I didn't have when I was younger."

Nancy admired Rhoda's dedication. It made her feel good to know that her father had helped Rhoda make River Arts possible.

"Can you join us for lunch?" Carson asked Rhoda, when they stepped out into the June sunshine a few moments later.

Rhoda shook her head as they all headed for the parking lot. "I have to get back with supplies for the art studios," she said, walking between two rows of parked cars. "Things are crazy busy these first few days. I really shouldn't have taken the time to visit, but—"

She stopped in her tracks. The joyful spark in her eyes darkened to a look of total shock. "My car!" she exclaimed.

Nancy turned to stare at the green minivan right next to them, and her mouth fell open.

Someone had spray-painted a message across the side of the van in dripping, bloodred letters:

"R.A. WILL GO DOWN. AND SO WILL YOU."

2

Arts and Threats

For a long moment no one spoke. Nancy felt a knot of dread twist inside her as she stared at the message. The steady drone of bulldozers and cranes from the construction site only made the feeling worse.

"Someone is threatening to ruin River Arts?" Carson said, breaking the silence. He turned to Rhoda with concern. "Has there been any trouble?"

Rhoda stood frowning at the message before she answered. "I got a note in the mail yesterday. I thought it was some kind of joke, but . . ."

She reached into her shoulder bag, pulled out an envelope, and extracted a folded piece of paper. She shook it open with a flip of her wrist, revealing a note made from letters that had been cut from magazines.

"'You'll get what you deserve.'" Nancy read the message out loud.

"Whoa!" Bess let out a low whistle. "That doesn't sound like a joke to me. Someone really has it in for you, Rhoda."

"Why didn't you tell me about this before?" Carson asked.

"I didn't think it was serious," Rhoda replied. "I mean, why would anyone want to hurt me or River Arts?"

"It sounds as if whoever sent this wants to get back at you for something," Nancy said, reading the note a second time. "Can you think of anyone with a grudge against you?"

Rhoda shrugged, fingering the turquoise beads of her necklace. "Starting River Arts has been a big job. I had to establish a board of directors, hire teachers, evaluate student records, renovate old buildings, and have new ones built," she said. "I'm sure there are people who didn't agree with some of the decisions I've made. But enemies?" She shook her head. "I can't think of anyone who would—"

All of a sudden she stopped and stared at something behind Nancy. "Wait a minute," Rhoda said, her eyes narrowing. "Bruce Pennington!"

"Who?" Nancy and Bess asked together.

Rhoda gave no sign that she'd heard them. "That weasel. *He* must have done this," she said.

She strode angrily toward the construction site, which edged the far side of the parking lot. Through an opening in the wooden barrier Nancy spotted two men wearing suits and hard hats. They stood poring over a blueprint, near a sign that read, This Site Being Developed by BP Ventures.

"One of those guys must be Bruce Pennington," Nancy said.

"Whoever *he* is," Bess replied.

"Bruce Pennington is Marianna's nephew. BP Ventures is his real estate development company," Carson told them. "I remember hearing that he was unhappy about Marianna's decision to turn the estate into an arts colony."

"Unhappy enough to threaten Rhoda?" Nancy moved automatically across the parking lot, following Rhoda. "Come on. She might need our help."

They reached the opening in the wooden barrier just as Rhoda stepped up to the two men. "How dare you threaten me, Bruce!" Rhoda said.

She jabbed her forefinger against the suit jacket of the taller of the two men. He was about her father's age, Nancy guessed, with short brown hair that was barely visible beneath his hard hat. Above his loosened tie and shirt collar, his neck and face were red and sweaty from the heat of the machines. He stepped back from Rhoda, his eyes shifting quickly to take in Carson, Nancy, and Bess.

"It's nice to see you, too, Rhoda," Bruce said sarcastically. "What's the problem? Taking my aunt's estate out from under me wasn't enough for you? You've got to come pester me here, too?"

He was angry all right, Nancy thought. There was a hard edge to his voice, and his eyes cut through Rhoda like steel blades. Stepping up beside Rhoda, Nancy said, "Someone's been sending threats to Rhoda."

"Including a spray-painted one on her car just now," Bess said hotly.

"Oh, really?" Bruce let out a sharp laugh. "Now, that's what I call good art," he said.

Nancy couldn't believe the arrogant satisfaction in his voice. What a jerk! To judge by the look on her father's face, he agreed with her.

"Threats are no laughing matter," Carson said.

"Everyone knows you were against River Arts from the beginning," Rhoda told Bruce. "If I find out you've been threatening me . . ."

Bruce drew himself up, looking indignant. "I'm shocked that you would suspect me, Rhoda. Truly shocked," he said, in a voice that was anything but sincere. "Besides, there's something you seem to be missing."

"What's that?" Bess wanted to know.

Bruce didn't answer right away. He reached into his jacket pocket, pulled out a candy, and twisted off the red-and-white wrapper. He tossed the wrapper to the ground before popping the candy into his mouth.

"Proof, Rhoda. That's what you're missing," he said. "Without it, your accusations don't mean a thing."

With that, he turned and rejoined the other man, who was waiting with the blueprint a few yards away.

Nancy watched the candy wrapper, bright red with a white zigzag around it, flip end over end as the wind blew it across the dirt. Bruce had a point, she thought. They *did* need proof. She quickly scanned the building site for a can of spray paint, then let out a sigh.

"Well," she said, "if Bruce spray-painted your van, he wasn't stupid enough to leave the can lying out in the open."

"Of course not. But it *had* to be him. Who else could have done it?" said Rhoda. She started back toward the parking lot, her feet kicking up clouds of dust.

As the others followed, Carson said, "The threats are worrisome, but I'm even more concerned about what might happen if the person who made those threats is serious."

"You mean"—Bess glanced worriedly from Carson to Nancy to Rhoda—"you think someone might really try to hurt Rhoda or River Arts?"

"I wouldn't have thought it was possible," said Rhoda. "But now . . ." She stopped next to the dripping red message that covered her car. "I'll admit I'm a little worried."

"Maybe I can help," Nancy said.

"And me!" Bess piped up.

Rhoda looked doubtful. Before she could object, Nancy said quickly, "We could stay at River Arts for a few days, just to keep our eyes open for anything suspicious."

"You won't find anyone better at getting to the bottom of a mystery," Carson said, with a proud glance at Nancy.

"Well, my intern *did* cancel at the last minute," Rhoda said. "I guess I could use the extra help—and the extra eyes—if you don't mind being put to work at River Arts, that is."

"Not at all," Bess said. She raised a hand to give Nancy a high five. "We'll be under cover and on the alert for trouble."

Nancy nodded, glancing back toward the construction site. "If Bruce Pennington, or anyone else, tries something, we'll be there to make sure he doesn't succeed."

"Am I dreaming?" Bess said as Nancy drove through the entrance to River Arts the next morning. "This place is too beautiful to be real!"

"Wow!" was all Nancy could say.

They hadn't been able to see much from the road outside, just the high stone wall surrounding the property and the leafy trees that rose above it. Now that they had passed beneath the arched stone entrance, Nancy was awestruck. She pulled the car off to the side and stopped so that she and Bess could take a long look.

The first thing that impressed Nancy was the house. It was one of the grandest places she had ever seen: three stories high, with graceful pillars, a slate patio, two wide wings that stretched left and right from the center, and a stone fountain out front. A wide lawn spread out from the house on three sides, while woods edged in close to the back. Paths seemed to wander off in all directions, and Nancy saw the corners of buildings and roofs nestled behind trees and shrubs. Flowering azaleas and rhododendrons were everywhere, along with modern sculptures of different colors and materials.

"No wonder Mrs. Pennington didn't want to give up this place," Nancy said. "It's amazing."

She was about to pull back into the road when she saw Rhoda heading their way across the lawn. With her was a slender girl about Nancy's age who wore shorts and a striped halter top.

"Nancy! Bess! Welcome," Rhoda greeted them. "I'm so happy you've arrived. Things have been so busy here I sure can use your help."

Nancy caught the warning look in Rhoda's eyes, and she understood the message: She and Bess had to be careful not to blow their cover as her interns.

"That's what we're here for," Bess said carefully. "When do we start working?"

"After you get the grand tour of River Arts," said the girl with Rhoda. Now that she was right near them, Nancy saw that she had bright green eyes, cheeks sprinkled with freckles, and jet black hair that fell around her face in curls. She shook hands with Nancy and Bess. "My name's Rosie Mallory. Rhoda asked me to show you around and help you get settled."

"Rosie is a dance student," Rhoda told them. "She'll show you where your room is and give you the four-one-one on River Arts. Once you've had a chance to settle in, stop by my office in the main house, and I'll put you right to work."

"Sounds good," Nancy replied.

"We'd better start the tour with the parking lot," Rosie said. "It isn't exactly the most scenic part of River Arts, but it's the only place here where cars are allowed. Mind if I hop in?"

Moments later Rosie was in the backseat, directing Nancy along a drive that forked right from the road that led to the house. They curved around to a gravel lot surrounded by woods. About fifteen cars were parked there. As soon as Nancy parked, Rosie jumped out.

"Rhoda didn't want a bunch of cars out front to wreck the beauty of River Arts, so she made sure the lot was tucked out of sight," Rosie commented. "Actually, it's closer to everything than you'd think."

Nancy noticed a few different paths that snaked into the woods and asked Rosie where they led.

"Those are shortcuts to the dance studios, the house, and the drama center," Rosie said. She pointed to a path just a few feet from where they were parked. "We'll take that one to get to the house. Fifty yards through the woods, and we're there."

Nancy looked around as she went to the trunk to get her bags. She spotted Rhoda's green minivan right away, parked at the far end of the lot. The spray-painted message had already been covered with a fresh coat of green paint, and—

Nancy blinked as a flash of movement next to the minivan caught her eye.

It was a man, she realized. She glimpsed dark hair and a work apron as the man stepped around from the far side of the van. He appeared to be circling it, peering through the windows as he went.

"What's he up to?" Nancy wondered aloud.

Rosie turned toward the minivan. When she saw the man, her face lit up. "Dad!" she called.

The man straightened up with a start. He looked quickly from Rosie to Nancy and Bess. "Um, hi, Rosie," he said. "Catch you later, okay?"

Without waiting for her answer, he turned and disappeared into the woods.

Rosie's smile faded on her lips. "I guess . . . he has something he has to do," she said uncertainly.

Or something to hide, Nancy thought. Keeping her voice light, she asked, "Is your father a teacher here?"

"He's the cook," Rosie answered distractedly, still gazing at the path down which her father had gone. "I wonder why . . ." Then she shook herself and turned back to Nancy and Bess. "I'll help you carry your bags."

Nancy and Bess exchanged a quick glance as they followed Rosie down the path she'd shown them. She obviously didn't want to talk about her father. But Nancy had to find out more—like why he was sneaking around Rhoda's minivan and whether he held a grudge against Rhoda.

"So, how do you and your dad like it here at River Arts?" Nancy asked.

Rosie hoisted the straps of Bess's backpack higher on her shoulders. "River Arts is a great place." She smiled back at Nancy. "I can't believe how lucky I am to—"

At that moment a loud crash echoed from somewhere ahead, making the three girls jump.

"What was that?" Bess exclaimed.

Before Nancy could answer, she heard voices shouting. She couldn't make out any words, but there was no mistaking the angry, bitter tone.

"Sounds like trouble," she said. Grabbing the straps of her bag more tightly, she broke into a run.

Rosie had already sprinted ahead. "I think it's coming from the house," she said.

As they ran, their bags banged against their bodies. The sounds of their footsteps and heavy breathing mixed with the shouts from ahead. A moment later they burst from the woods into the blinding sunshine.

They were behind the big house, Nancy saw, next to a wide slate patio dotted with furniture and potted flowers and plants. Sunlight glinted off the back windows of the house, but Nancy was able to make out a TV that lay smashed on the patio. Shattered glass, twisted metal, and busted electronic components mixed with the broken plaster, earth, and the smashed fern leaves of the planter on which the television had fallen.

"Someone must have thrown it out of the house," Bess said, stopping at the edge of the patio.

Nancy, Bess, and Rosie weren't the only ones who had heard the crash. Half a dozen other people were running from all directions. All of them stared curiously at the third-floor window directly above the broken television. Nancy couldn't see the two people arguing inside, but she—and everybody else—could still hear them.

"Shouldn't someone go up there to try to stop the

fight?" Nancy asked. "I mean, what if they—"

"Aiiiii!"

A shriek rang out from the third-floor window. The hollow, terrified sound chilled Nancy.

In the next instant a body was pushed through the window. Arms and legs flailing, it plummeted toward the patio.

3

A Performance to Die For

"Noooo!" Nancy cried.

She dropped her bags and sprinted forward—but not fast enough. The person hit the slate tiles with a sickening thud before Nancy or anyone could do anything to break the fall.

Cries and gasps of horror sounded from behind her.

"Call nine-one-one!" Nancy yelled over her shoulder. "Someone go inside to find the person who . . ."

Her voice trailed off as she studied the victim for the first time. "Hey! This isn't a real person," she said. "It's a dummy!"

The dummy was made of a spongy material covered with skin-colored cloth. It had been dressed in blue jeans, a long-sleeved shirt, and sneakers. A hat was pulled low over its face.

"I don't get it," Bess said, coming up next to Nancy. "Why would—"

"Smile, everyone." A voice floated down from above. "You're on *Candid Camera!*"

Nancy looked up to see two guys leaning out the third-floor window with big grins on their faces. The one on the left had light brown skin, a round face, and hair bleached blond with the roots showing. The other was fair-skinned, with straight natural blond hair long enough to tuck behind his ears and a face that was mostly hidden behind the video camera he held. He aimed the camera down at everyone clustered around the dummy on the patio.

"We really got you that time," he said, laughing.

"You mean, you guys pulled this as a *stunt*?" Rosie asked. "I nearly had a heart attack!"

The boy with the bleached hair shrugged. "Hey, performance art should make an impact, right? If it doesn't shock, it's not worth doing."

Rosie rolled her eyes. Keeping her voice low, she told Nancy and Bess, "That's Marco Rivera. He's here to study performance art. That other guy, the one with the camera, is Marco's roommate, TJ Peters."

"Let me guess. He's a video arts student?" said Bess.

"Yup," Rosie answered. "I'm not sure what kinds of projects they're working on with their teachers. Mostly it seems they just try to trick everyone with practical jokes like this."

Nancy wasn't sure what she thought of the boys' performance. But one thing was certain: Not everyone appreciated being duped by the falling dummy. She saw a red-haired boy wearing paint-stained shorts and a T-shirt scowl up at Marco.

"Who said you could take my TV?" the boy demanded.

"It doesn't work, Stu," Marco replied. "What's the big deal?"

Nancy couldn't believe how arrogant and irresponsible Marco sounded. Stu started to answer him, but he stopped as a white-haired woman hustled onto the patio in denim pants, a sleeveless shirt, a wide-brimmed straw hat, and flowered gardening gloves. Her wrinkled skin had the ruddy coloring of someone who spent a lot of time outdoors.

"You two, up there!" she called sternly, tilting her head up to gaze at Marco and TJ. Her alert gray eyes flashed with annoyance. "Damaging other people's property is serious business. I'll have you know you owe me a new planter. And if any of my slate tiles are cracked, I expect you to replace them."

Marco and TJ looked at each other. "So, we wrecked a few old things, Mrs. Pennington," Marco said.

Nancy shot the white-haired woman a second glance. So *this* was Marianna Pennington. She seemed like a determined person, but Marco wasn't treating her—or anyone else—with much respect.

"What we made is cutting edge performance art." Marco went on with a smug grin. "That's worth a lot more than some old stuff."

"That's enough, Marco." Rhoda spoke up from the French doors that led into the house.

Nancy hadn't even realized Rhoda was there. Rhoda stepped out onto the deck and surveyed the heap of plaster, dirt, and components.

"Mrs. Pennington," she said, "I'll make sure Marco and TJ clean up and replace anything they've damaged." She frowned up at the two boys and raised her voice. "But first I'd like to see you both in my office. You've taken performance art too far this time."

Nancy expected the boys to apologize. Instead Marco glared at Rhoda before stepping away from the window and out of sight.

"Did you see that look?" Bess whispered. "Marco smashes up half the patio and scares everyone to death. Now he acts as if *he's* the one being treated unfairly."

"Mmm." Nancy squinted at the mess Marco and TJ had left behind. Marco obviously didn't mind wrecking other people's property. Also, if that glare he'd given Rhoda was any indication, he wasn't exactly her biggest fan.

Nancy shook herself. Don't jump to conclusions, she thought. One angry look and an irresponsible attitude were hardly proof that Marco had spray-painted Rhoda's minivan or sent her that threat in the mail.

Still, Nancy thought, I'm going to keep an eye on him from now on.

"Well," Bess said an hour later, "we've seen the art studios, the performance and dance studios, the sculpture garden, the drama center, the rose garden, and now this!"

She leaned against the railing of a gazebo at the very edge of River Arts. An ivy-covered stone wall ran left and right along a cliff top that overlooked the Muskoka River far below. Behind them, the lawn stretched to the main house like a carpet of green velvet. Woods crowded close to the cliffs on both sides, as well as across the river. Except for the River Arts buildings and a bridge that crossed the Muskoka to the south, there was hardly any sign that people inhabited the area.

"The view is amazing," Nancy said.

"We're not done yet." With a smile, Rosie stepped off the gazebo and headed toward the woods to their right. "The River Arts theater-in-the-round is this way. After that, I'll give you an inside tour of the most important place of all."

Bess raised a questioning eyebrow. "What could be better than what we've seen already?" she asked.

"The kitchen! We artsy types burn up a lot of calories when we work," Rosie said. "Luckily, my dad is a good cook. The food here is fantastic."

She laughed, but Nancy grew quiet at the mention

of Rosie's dad. She hadn't forgotten the suspicious way he'd acted in the parking lot. Now, as Rosie led the way through the woods, Nancy replayed the scene in her mind. She barely paid attention to the stone theater in a clearing in the woods that Rosie showed Bess and her. She was glad when Rosie headed back toward the main house. At last she and Bess would have a chance to find out more about Rosie's dad.

Rosie led them through the main entrance of the house. Nancy and Bess had briefly been through it before their tour, to drop off their bags in the first-floor bedroom they would share in the north wing of the house. This time Rosie bypassed the hallway that led to the students' rooms. Instead she went through a huge dining room to the kitchen at the back of the house.

Her father stood before a butcher-block counter, surrounded by onions, peppers, tomatoes, and mushrooms, which he was chopping. The scents of fresh herbs and garlic filled the air. Rosie's father reached over to stir something that was simmering on the stainless steel stove, then jumped when Rosie called his name.

He blinked in surprise, then smiled and said, "Oh, it's you, Rosie. You've come for a visit?"

"Absolutely," Rosie told him. "Bess, Nancy, this is my dad, Shane Mallory."

Nancy took a long look at Shane. He was in his

forties, she guessed, with a tall, stocky build and the same pale skin and dark hair as Rosie. However, while Rosie's eyes were green, Shane's were cloudy blue, and they kept shifting distractedly. He smiled at Nancy and Bess, but his jaw seemed tense.

"I was going to introduce Bess and Nancy before, when we saw you in the parking lot. But . . . well, you seemed kind of busy." Rosie bit her lip, then said, "What was going on? You barely even talked to me."

Yes! Nancy thought. It was exactly the question she wanted to ask.

Shane kept his eyes on the chopping block. He took a shiny metal pocketknife from his pocket and used it to cut the string around some parsley.

"You know I can't always talk when I'm working," he said.

A doubtful glimmer came into Bess's eyes, and Nancy thought she understood why. Shane hadn't looked as if he'd been working when they saw him. He'd looked as if he were snooping.

If Rosie thought her dad's response was odd, she didn't say so. She watched him cut away pepper stems for a moment longer, then frowned slightly and said, "Well, I guess we'll be going. You're going to watch *West Side Story* with me tonight, right?"

"*West Side Story*?" Bess echoed, grinning. "I *love* that movie!"

"We're having an outdoor showing tonight on the

27

lawn," Rosie said. She spoke to Bess, but Nancy noticed that Rosie's eyes stayed on her father. "Dad?" she said, prompting him.

"Hmm? Oh, I'll be there," Shane replied. He barely nodded as they said goodbye. The tension never left his face for a second.

What's up with him? Nancy wondered.

"Your dad seems kind of distracted," Bess commented to Rosie, as they made their way back through the dining room.

That was the understatement of the year, thought Nancy. "Is everything all right?" she asked.

Rosie gave a halfhearted smile. "I guess so. The truth is, I don't really know my dad that well yet," she said. "He and Mom got divorced when I was a baby. I grew up with my mom on the East Coast, and Dad was always traveling for work. He was a cook on a cruise ship for years, so I hardly ever saw him."

She paused for a moment, tugging one of her black curls. "I was really psyched when Dad told me he was working at River Arts and sent me an application," Rosie said. "He said he wanted to spend more time with me. You know, so we could get to know each other. It was great for the first couple of days, but now . . . I don't know, he's in a bad mood, and he can't seem to spare a single second for me."

As Nancy listened, a question popped into her head. Was it coincidence that Shane's bad mood had kicked in at the same time Rhoda began to receive threats?

"Maybe he doesn't like River Arts as much as he thought he would," Nancy suggested. "How does he like working for Rhoda?"

"No problem there. Dad and Rhoda are friends," Rosie answered right away. "That's how he got the job here in the first place."

Hmm, thought Nancy. If Shane and Rhoda were friends, it seemed unlikely that he would threaten her. Still, he had been so gruff and *un*welcoming. And the way he hadn't answered Rosie's question about what he was up to in the parking lot . . .

Nancy sighed. Shane was hiding something; she could feel it. If only she could find out what and why.

"You suspect Shane?" Rhoda asked a few hours later. She looked up from a wood and metal sculpture that she, Nancy, and Bess had just positioned in the sculpture garden.

The late-afternoon sun sent long shadows across the grass. Nancy and Bess had wanted to speak to Rhoda about Shane earlier, but as Rhoda's "interns" they had been sent on half a dozen errands. Until Rhoda asked them to help her install her newest sculpture—made of rods, spheres, and other geometric shapes that shifted in the wind—they hadn't had a moment alone with her.

"He *was* nosing around your van," Nancy said.

"Shane wouldn't do anything to hurt me *or* River

29

Arts," Rhoda replied, shaking her head firmly.

Nancy used a wrench to tighten one of the bolts that attached the sculpture to its metal base. "Do you have any idea why he's so tense and aloof?" she asked.

"Shane has always been private. I don't think you should confuse that with guilt," Rhoda said. She finished tightening the other bolts, then stepped back to survey the sculpture. "Anyway, how do we even know those threats were serious? Whoever made them hasn't done anything to follow through."

Nancy hoped Rhoda was right, but she wasn't going to count on it. While Rhoda examined her sculpture, Nancy took a small notebook and pen from the backpack she had brought with her. Quickly she wrote down Shane's name and Marco's, along with the reasons she suspected them.

"Please don't get everyone at River Arts alarmed," Rhoda told her. "Most people here don't know about the threats, and I'd like to keep it that way. That's why I had the one on the van painted over right away yesterday. I want everyone to concentrate on work, not get all caught up in some cloak-and-dagger routine."

"But you want us to be on the lookout for trouble, right?" Bess asked. She took the tools from Nancy and Rhoda and dropped them into the toolbox they'd brought with them.

"Of course," Rhoda replied. "But I'm telling you, if there *is* trouble, Shane is not the person who's causing it."

They started back toward the house, passing a series of red pyramids, a sculpture of fanciful curlicues, and a bronze sculpture that resembled a horse. Nancy was lost in thought as they circled past a long building studded with windows. She remembered from their tour that this was where the art studios were.

"What about Marco?" she asked Rhoda. "He sure seems to resent your authority."

"Marco reminds me a lot of me when I was younger," Rhoda said, laughing. "He's really got an attitude when it comes to—"

All of a sudden, she stopped talking and shaded her eyes from the sun. "What on earth—?"

Ahead of them, half a dozen easels were set up on the lawn that sloped up toward the main house. Nancy thought she recognized some of the painting students she and Bess had met during their tour earlier. They were clustered around two women who were arguing.

"Isn't that the painting teacher?" Bess asked, pointing at the taller of the two women. She was in her late twenties, had blond hair pulled back in a French braid, and wore a paint-splattered apron.

"Susan Gimble," Rhoda said, nodding.

Susan looked anything but happy. She was gesturing angrily at the easels. "You can't hold a landscape painting class here," Nancy heard her say to the other woman. "You're not even a teacher at River Arts!"

The other woman, who was slightly older—in her midthirties—had short, sleek dark hair, a curvy figure, and a face filled with determination. Ignoring Susan completely, she turned to the students and said, "Let's get started, shall we? I want each of you to choose an easel and the view you'd like to paint."

"I can't believe she's here again," Rhoda said under her breath.

"Who?" Nancy asked.

"Gemma Vance," Rhoda answered, her brow wrinkling. "She applied for a job teaching painting here. I guess she's having a hard time accepting the fact that the board hired Susan instead of her."

With a frustrated roll of her eyes, Rhoda strode over to the woman. "I know you're disappointed that your application to teach wasn't accepted, Ms. Vance," she said, "but—"

"Please!" The woman held up a hand filled with paintbrushes. "No interruptions. I'm busy conducting a class."

"Susan Gimble teaches all the painting classes here at River Arts," Rhoda said firmly. "I'm afraid I'll have to ask you to leave."

Gemma made no move. Nancy couldn't believe

how nervy she was. "I am a much better painting teacher than anyone else you'll find," Gemma said. "You'll see."

"What's her problem?" Bess whispered. "Why won't she take no for an answer?"

Nancy was glad to see that Rhoda didn't back down. "I'll be forced to call the police if you don't leave," Rhoda told Gemma.

For the first time Gemma's determined gaze faltered. "Y-you wouldn't dare," she said.

"Care to test me?" Rhoda asked.

Nancy looked back and forth between the two women. The tension was so electric that she half expected to see sparks. It seemed like an eternity before Gemma finally said, "Fine. I'll leave."

At that moment a whiff of smoke tickled Nancy's nostrils. She turned, taking in the green hillside, flowering rhododendrons, and—

"Oh, no!" She gasped as her gaze fell on the building that housed the art studios. Smoke poured from the high windows, and the glass glowed an ominous yellow-orange.

"The studios," she said. "They're on fire!"

4

Fire!

"There could be people in there. We have to do something!" Bess cried.

Nancy was already on the move. She raced across the lawn toward the studios. Shocked exclamations rang in the air, followed by the sounds of people racing down the grassy slope behind her.

"I'll call the fire department," Rhoda called out.

Nancy didn't turn or look. Every ounce of her attention was focused on the building at the bottom of the hill. Her eyes searched from window to window, for any movement. She strained to hear calls for help. There was just dense smoke and crackling flames, growing thicker and louder every second.

"I'm here, Nan!" Bess's breathless voice came from right behind Nancy.

34

Nancy nodded to show she'd heard. She zeroed in on the door to the studio building. Heart pounding, she ran the last few yards, then stopped outside the door.

A thick plume of smoke billowed through the opening, making her eyes sting. She tried to wave it away to look inside. "The wood's not too hot," she told Bess, pressing her hand against the outside of the door. "The fire must be on the other side of the building."

Nancy pulled the door open, and she and Bess stepped inside. A thick wall of heat and smoke hit them, making them double over in fits of coughing.

"Ugh!" Bess cried. Her hands flew to her mouth and nose. "I can't see a thing! How are we going to—"

All of a sudden Nancy felt a wet shower hit her from above. Blinking furiously, she tried to see through the hot, stinging smoke.

"Sprinklers!" she exclaimed.

"It's about time they turned on," someone muttered behind them.

Turning, Nancy saw Susan Gimble's red, sweat-streaked face through the smoke. Coughing, Susan pushed past Nancy and headed to the left of the door. "The sinks are over here," she said. "And some buckets. Let's get to work!"

The next ten minutes passed in a hot, smoky blur. When Nancy, Bess, and Susan finally emerged from the building, the fire was out. Soaking wet and covered with sooty grit, they collapsed onto the grass outside. A crowd had gathered, but Nancy was so busy gulping for air that she didn't pay much attention to them at first.

"Thank goodness no one was inside," Bess said, taking in heaving breaths of air.

"That's a relief." Rhoda stepped forward and bent down next to Nancy, Bess, and Susan. "I'm sorry I couldn't run as fast as you could. Are you all right? I've sent for the doctor from the infirmary. I want him to check you three out right away."

Nancy frowned. "*After* I take a look around," she said, propping herself up on her elbows. "We were so busy putting the fire out, there wasn't a chance to find out how it started."

The inside of the building was a mess. Art studios were situated along both sides of the long structure, separated from one another by partitions. Paintings, partitions, and supplies were soaking wet and covered with dripping, sooty stains. A burned, smoky smell hung in the air.

"Just when the students were really starting to get into their projects," Susan said, following Nancy, Rhoda, and Bess into the building, "this has to happen."

Nancy noticed that most of the damage was from smoke and the sprinklers. Only one studio, at the far end of the building, looked as if it had actually been on fire.

"The fire must have started down there," she said.

Quickly they made their way down the central corridor toward the burned studio. Bess didn't say anything, but Nancy saw the sober glint in her eyes as she looked at the charred partition and peeling, burned canvas hanging on it.

"Hey!" Bess dropped to her knees at a heap of burned rags on the floor next to the most badly burned part of the partition. Alongside it were the charred remains of an oblong metal container. "Is this what I think it is?" Bess asked.

Nancy bent down and sniffed the can. "Turpentine," she said.

She pointed to the mound of rags next to the can. Most of them were burned beyond recognition, but Nancy plucked out a corner of red paisley fabric. "It's a bandanna," she said. "It looks as if there was a whole pile of them." She held the bit of fabric close to her nose and frowned. "They've been soaked in turpentine."

"Whose studio is this?" Rhoda asked.

"Stu Evans's," Susan answered. "I saw him outside just now."

She left the building and returned a moment later with the red-haired young man whose television set Marco had ruined. Stu looked at his studio with wide, shocked eyes before turning to the pile of charred bandannas Susan showed him.

"Bandannas?" Stu looked up at Susan in surprise. "How did those get there?"

"They're not yours?" Bess asked.

Stu shook his head. "No way. They definitely weren't here when I was working before. I mean, I'd just finished sweeping my studio floor when that lady showed up to teach landscape painting."

"Gemma Vance?" Nancy asked, her fingers tightening on the bit of red cloth. "*She* was here?"

"Sure," Stu answered. "She made us all drop what we were doing so we could take her landscape painting class."

Coincidence? Nancy wondered. Somehow she doubted it. "Let's talk to her," she said. She started toward the door, but Rhoda caught her arm.

"She's gone," Rhoda said. "She packed up and left while I was calling the fire department."

Sure enough, when Nancy went back outside and looked around, she didn't see Gemma. The hillside appeared empty except for two people who were hurrying down the hill toward them. Nancy recognized Rosie's slender figure in a dance leotard, and her father's stockier frame.

"I just heard what happened," Rosie said. "Is everyone all right?"

"No one's hurt, if that's what you mean," Susan

told her. She turned as Rhoda and Bess came out of the studio building behind her. "Shouldn't we call the police?" Susan asked.

"Police?" Shane echoed. His face went white, and his jaw clenched tight.

"No need to worry, everyone," Rhoda said quickly. "I'm sure we can work this out on our own. Please go back to whatever you were doing."

She waited until people began moving away from the studio building before speaking to Nancy. "I'm not going to call the police, but I'll let the fire department know what we've found when they get here and hope that we don't get any bad publicity," she said in a low voice. "We don't need that."

Nancy noticed that Shane had hung behind. When he heard Rhoda, his expression relaxed a little. Still, Nancy didn't miss the way his eyes lingered on the studio building as he walked away.

"Hey," Bess said, breaking into Nancy's thoughts, "I just noticed something."

Nancy tore her gaze away from Shane. "What?" she asked.

"Well . . ." Bess bit her lip, staring after the people who moved up the grassy lawn away from the studio building. "It seems that just about everyone heard about the fire and came running," she said, "everyone except one person."

Nancy blinked as it hit her. "Marco," she said.

Shading her eyes from the sun, she scanned the hillside. TJ was there, carrying his video camera at his side. But Marco was nowhere in sight.

"Where could he be?" Bess wondered aloud.

"Add that to our list of questions about Gemma, Shane, *and* Marco," Nancy said. "I just hope we start getting some answers—soon."

"Marco's still missing in action," Bess said to Nancy as they stepped into the dining room awhile later.

Nancy scanned the room and again failed to find Marco. "It's seven now," she said, checking her watch. "It looks as if everyone else is here. I guess Rhoda wasn't kidding when she told us it was important to be on time."

The dining room had been set up for a buffet at lunchtime, with small groups of tables and chairs. For dinner the room had been completely transformed. The small tables had been replaced by a long oval table covered with a white damask tablecloth, flowers, and flickering candles. A bowl of spicy gazpacho soup was at every place, with baskets of crusty bread nearby. Just looking at the food made Nancy's stomach growl. She noticed that students and teachers remained standing.

"What are we waiting for?" Bess asked Rosie, who stood with a few other students just inside the doorway.

"Dinner is kind of formal," Rosie said. "We never sit down until Mrs. Pennington gets here."

Across the room Rhoda glanced at her watch. She walked over to Nancy and said, "It's not like Mrs. Pennington to be late. Would you mind reminding her about dinner?"

"No problem," Nancy told her.

She hurried from the dining room and made her way back to the entrance hall. During their tour Rosie had pointed out the wing where Marianna Pennington lived, on the opposite side of the house from where the student rooms were. A door led to it from the entrance hall.

"Hello?" Nancy called as she pushed open the door. "Mrs. Pennington?"

Stepping through the doorway, she found herself in a long hallway lined with doors. A window at the end of the hall glowed with early-evening light. To Nancy's right, stairs rose. Nancy couldn't see anyone, but she heard voices coming from a room just beyond the staircase.

"Mrs. Pennington?" she said again, moving down the hallway. "Is that—"

Nancy stopped short in the middle of the hall. The hairs at the back of her neck stood on end, and her skin tingled. She was struck with the sudden, overwhelming sensation that she was being watched.

Nancy turned quickly in every direction, but no

one was there. "Get a grip," she murmured. Shaking herself, she continued down the hall. Still, she couldn't rid herself of the unsettled feeling that had come over her.

"It's all *their* fault!" A man's voice burst from the room beyond the staircase.

Nancy hesitated. She knew that voice. It belonged to Bruce Pennington, and he didn't sound happy.

"Those kids set that fire, and you know it!" Bruce went on. "First the patio, now this. This whole place will be destroyed before they're through."

Marianna said something in a quiet voice Nancy couldn't hear clearly. Then Bruce's angry voice boomed out into the hallway again.

"I tried to protect you," he said. "I made sure the contract with River Arts specified that you could revoke the lease if they caused serious damage. If you don't revoke the lease after this, you're crazy!"

Nancy thought she heard Marianna try to say something, but Bruce steamrollered over her. "You could have made serious money with my plan to build luxury condos," he said. "Mark my words, Aunt Marianna, you're going to regret that decision. You're going to regret it big time."

Nancy heard heavy footsteps stomp across a carpet. A split second later Bruce burst into the hallway. His face was red, and his eyes flashed with anger.

He stopped short when he saw Nancy, and his

eyes narrowed to steely slits. They were like lasers that burned into her, making her shiver from head to toe.

"I, uh . . ." she began.

She didn't have a chance to say more. In the next instant Bruce stormed past Nancy, pushed through the door at the end of the hall, and was gone.

5

Sneaking Suspicions

"What was *that* all about?" Nancy muttered to herself.

She turned to observe Marianna Pennington step into the hallway. She had changed out of her gardening clothes and was wearing a dress that was the same silvery white as her hair. Seeing Nancy, Marianna paused and said, "Oh, my. I didn't realize anyone was here."

"Rhoda asked me to remind you about dinner," Nancy said. "I'm Nancy Drew. My friend Bess Marvin and I are Rhoda's interns."

"Yes, of course. Rhoda mentioned your names to me." Marianna gave Nancy a smile. "You'll have to excuse my nephew," she said. "Bruce gets worked up, but he doesn't mean any harm."

Nancy wished she could be sure of that. After hearing Bruce's outburst, she was troubled by a nagging suspicion. Bruce had said he'd made sure the contract with River Arts allowed Marianna to back out of the agreement if River Arts damaged her estate. He blamed the students for the fire, but Nancy had thought of another possibility. What if he was responsible? What if he had set the fire on purpose, hoping that his aunt would cancel the agreement with River Arts and go ahead with his plan to build condos?

"Mrs. Pennington," Nancy said, "was Bruce here for a long visit this afternoon?"

"Heavens, no!" Marianna said. "Bruce is always so tied up in his work that he never stays long. I don't think he was here longer than fifteen minutes."

"Oh." Nancy stifled a sigh. If what Marianna had said was true, Bruce couldn't have set the fire. "Well, I guess we'd better get to the dining room and—"

A noise behind them made Nancy stop. She whirled around and saw a flash of skin outside the window at the end of Marianna Pennington's private hall.

"Someone's there!" she said.

Nancy sprinted to the end of the hallway and leaned out the open window. She whipped her head left just in time to see a gray sneaker and a blur of black that looked as if it might be some kind of bag.

"Hey! Stop!" Nancy shouted.

Whoever it was disappeared around the corner of the house. Nancy intended to climb out the window to follow, but stopped when Marianna called out to her.

"What's going on out there?" Marianna asked. The older woman was standing a few feet away. Her hands were on her hips, and she was gazing curiously at Nancy.

"Someone was listening at the window," Nancy told her, "someone with gray sneakers and a black bag."

Marianna waved her tanned, wrinkled hand and said, "I am too old to worry about who listens to me and who doesn't. What's more important is that a roomful of hungry people are waiting for us to be able to eat. If we don't get to the dining room fast, we could have a rebellion on our hands."

"Well . . ." Nancy hesitated, taking a last look out the window. Then she started back toward the entrance hall with Marianna. "I guess I couldn't have caught up with whoever it was anyway," she said. "Besides, I'm starved!"

Apparently she wasn't the only one. Everyone in the dining room appeared relieved to see Marianna. As soon as she was seated at the head of the table, they all sat down and dug in. Nancy found a place between Bess and a slender man in his forties who had wide brown eyes, skin the color of milk choco-late, and the richest, deepest voice Nancy had ever heard. Across the table from them was an empty chair—Marco's, Nancy assumed. He still hadn't arrived for dinner.

"Hey, Nan," Bess whispered. She leaned close to Nancy, her eyes sparkling with excitement. "Guess what I found out from—"

At that moment Marco sauntered into the room. Nancy did a double take when she saw what he was wearing. "Gray sneakers!" she whispered. "And check out his sports bag."

Bess, reaching for a piece of bread, frowned. "Who cares what he's wearing? I found out that—"

"Ah, Mr. Rivera!" the man on Nancy's other side spoke up. "How nice of you to join us. When you failed to show up for our work session this afternoon, I feared you might be sick."

Nancy paused with her soup spoon in midair. "Marco missed his work session?" she whispered to Bess.

"That's what I've been trying to tell you," Bess whispered back. "I talked to Craig Harrison while you were gone." She nodded at the slender man be-side Nancy. "He's the performance arts teacher here. He was pretty steamed that Marco was a no-show."

Nancy's mind raced a mile a minute. Marco had missed his work session, and he hadn't been around after the fire. So where *had* he been? And why had he been eavesdropping at Mrs. Pennington's window?

Nancy watched Marco closely as he slipped the black bag under the empty chair across the table and sat down. "Sorry, Mr. H., but something came up," Marco said, shrugging. "You know how it is. Art doesn't always follow a schedule."

"Talk about a lame excuse," Bess said under her breath.

That was for sure, Nancy thought. She said to Marco, "I'd like to hear more about your acting."

"Me, too," Bess said, picking up on Nancy's comment. "It would be really cool to know how you work. I mean, did some kind of inspiration strike this afternoon? Maybe you could give us a blow-by-blow rundown of what happens when you get ideas for your performances."

Marco forked his fingers through his bleached hair. "What are you trying to do, take all the fun out of it?" he said. "My kind of performance is something you do, not something you talk about."

"Like looking through people's windows?" Nancy said. "Is that your kind of performance?"

For an instant Marco's eyes narrowed. He swallowed some soup before looking at Nancy again. "Anything could be my kind of performance," he said vaguely. "But I don't give previews. That would wreck the surprise."

Nancy kept up her questions. But ten minutes later, when Shane cleared the soup bowls and brought out huge platters of pasta, Marco still hadn't revealed anything about what he'd been up to that afternoon. He was good at sidestepping her, but Nancy wasn't about to give up.

If he can be sneaky, she thought, so can I.

"*West Side Story* is my absolute favorite movie," Bess commented later that evening. She sat back in one of the folding chairs that had been set up on the lawn outside the main house, in front of a movie screen that was more than fifteen feet high. "I can't wait for the scene where Tony and Maria first meet."

Nancy couldn't help smiling. Bess was the ultimate romantic, but Nancy had too much on her mind to pay attention to what was happening in the movie.

She scanned the faces around her in the flickering, reflected light from the screen. Rosie was there, Nancy saw. She sat with a few other students near the back.

"Didn't Shane say he was going to watch the movie with Rosie tonight?" Nancy said, thinking out loud.

Bess nodded. Tearing her gaze from the screen, she glanced at Rosie, then made a face. "He's not here, huh? I guess Rosie wasn't kidding when she

49

said he's been too distracted to spend much time with her."

"Mmm." Nancy resolved to be on the lookout for Shane, but there was something else she needed to do first.

"Marco and TJ are here," she whispered to Bess. She nodded toward some seats up front, where the two guys were sitting. "This is my chance to sneak into their room to see if I can find anything connecting them to the threats.

All of a sudden Nancy cocked her head to the side and stared into the darkness to their left. "I thought I saw something move," she murmured. "Yes—over there!"

It was a man, she saw. He was dressed in dark clothes, but his pale face glistened in the moonlight. The man skirted the edge of some trees, as if he didn't want to stand out. Even in the darkness, Nancy recognized his tall, stocky build.

"It's Shane," she said, feeling her muscles tighten. "He's heading down the hill toward the art studios."

In the glow from the screen, Bess's eyes shone with concern. "No way," she said.

"I know Rhoda trusts Shane, but"—Nancy was already on her feet—"why is he sneaking around like that?"

"There's one way to find out," Bess said. With a grin she followed Nancy toward the trees. "Anyway,

I've seen *West Side Story* a zillion times."

Up ahead Shane was just disappearing around a thick knot of rhododendron bushes. Nancy picked up the pace, moving down the hillside along the edge of the woods. "Quick!" she whispered. "I don't want to lose him or give him enough time to do any damage."

She hurried around the side of the bushes, then stopped, inspecting the area.

Shane was gone from sight.

"Where *is* he?" she muttered.

Behind them the sound track from the movie swelled into a song. The melody hung eerily in the air as Nancy stared at the black, boxy silhouette of the art studio building. Except for the windows, which shone in the light from the crescent moon above, the building was completely dark.

"Do you think he's in there?" Bess whispered, coming up behind Nancy. "It's got to smell gross after the fire today."

Nancy's eyes examined every inch of the building and the area nearby. She didn't see any movement.

"I don't know," she said, swallowing her frustration. "He's got to be somewhere around here."

Moving as silently as they could, Nancy and Bess continued toward the studio building. Nancy looked left and right, on the alert for any movement.

"The door's open!" Bess whispered as they got closer to the building. "He must be in—"

Bang! A clang rang out, making Nancy jump about a foot in the air. "That came from somewhere past the studio," she said.

"You mean, where the sculpture garden is?" Bess asked. "That must be where Shane went!"

Nancy didn't waste a second. She raced past the art building, with Bess right behind her. As soon as they rounded the far corner of the building, the shadowy shapes of the sculpture garden came into sight in the distance. Nancy could make out the triangular shadows of the pyramids and the distinctive bronze horse. But the rest of it . . .

"It's hard to tell what's a sculpture," Nancy said, "and what's a tree or a—"

"There!" Bess cried, pointing. "Next to Rhoda's new sculpture."

Nancy's eyes flew to the spot where they had installed the sculpture that afternoon. The geometric shapes hung like dark shadows over the base. Sure enough, right next to them was the jet black silhouette of a person.

Nancy gasped as the person raised something high in the air. "A sledgehammer!" she said, then shouted, "Stop!"

Even as she screamed the word, Nancy saw the sledgehammer being swung downward. It smashed into the sculpture with a splintering crack that chilled her.

6

A Chase Through the Woods

Anger boiled up inside Nancy. "Oh no, you don't," she said under her breath as the person lifted the sledgehammer yet again.

"Hey, you! Stop!" Bess shouted, cupping her hands around her mouth.

For a brief instant, the silhouette froze. Then Nancy saw the sledgehammer drop to the ground. There was a black streak as the person took off toward the trees beyond the sculpture garden.

"He's heading for the woods!" Nancy cried, sprinting ahead. "We've got to catch him!"

She could hear Bess behind her, panting as they pounded across the grass. But Nancy didn't dare take her eyes off the dark silhouette.

"Come on, Drew," she urged herself out loud.

Gritting her teeth, she poured on more speed. The sculptures were a series of dark blurs as Nancy and Bess whizzed past them. Nancy's heart thumped, but she kept her eyes on the silhouette ahead, and marked the exact spot where it had disappeared into the woods.

"This way!" Nancy angled left and raced between two trees.

A dense blackness enveloped her immediately. Goose bumps popped out all over her arms and legs, but Nancy made herself keep running.

"I can't see a thing!" Bess called behind her.

After reaching into the pocket of her jeans, Nancy took out her penlight and clicked it on. The beam barely lit up a dizzying blur of branches, leaves, and tree trunks, and it wasn't strong enough to reach the person they were chasing.

"Try to follow my penlight," Nancy told Bess. "We're getting closer."

The sounds of snapping branches and crackling leaves weren't far ahead now. As Nancy followed, branches seemed to leap out to whip her arms and legs and grab at her clothes. Every root jumped from the ground to trip her. Nancy yanked her T-shirt free of a branch and then started running again.

That was when she heard it: the metallic thunk of a car door closing, followed by the roar of an engine.

"A car?" Bess said breathlessly. "Here?"

Nancy didn't answer. She had no explanation.

"Ouch!" Nancy winced as some thorns scratched her arms and legs. She pushed past some prickly bushes, then stopped short, blinking madly.

She had reached a break in the woods where some sort of dirt road cut through the trees. She could see two dirt tracks, with the gangly branches of berry bushes crowding close on both sides. A narrow strip of sky framed the crescent moon above. To her left the sound of the car engine grew fainter.

Gulping in air, Nancy turned in time to see two red taillights fading in the distance.

"I . . . can't believe he . . . got away," Bess said, coming up to Nancy. She doubled over, resting her hands on her knees while she caught her breath.

"Or she," Nancy said. "We can't be sure the person was Shane." She looked right, squinting into the darkness. At the end of the lane she saw the dark silhouette of the ivy-covered stone wall that edged the cliff. The sound of rushing water came from beyond it. "That's the cliff by the river," she said. "Maybe we should follow this road the other way to see where—"

"Hey!" Bess interrupted her. She straightened up, holding a crumpled square of red cellophane that glistened in the faint moonlight. "Recognize this?"

The cellophane crinkled as Nancy took it between her fingers and shone her penlight on it. She angled the beam along the distinctive white line that zigzagged across the bright red wrapper. "It's a candy wrapper," she said, "from the same kind of candy Bruce Pennington had when we saw him at the construction site yesterday."

"So . . ." Bess stared down the rutted lane where the red taillights had faded to black. "You think *he* smashed Rhoda's sculpture?"

"It sure seems like it," Nancy answered. She rolled the candy wrapper between her fingers, trying to make sense of all that had just happened. "But if that was Bruce, then where's Shane? What's *he* been up to this whole time?"

"At least now we know where this dirt road leads," Nancy said ten minutes later.

She and Bess stepped off the dirt track onto a paved road. Streetlights positioned along both sides of the road cast a yellow glow.

"It's the road we took to get to River Arts," Bess said. She nodded at the stone arch that marked the entrance to the arts colony, about fifty yards up the road. "Funny, I didn't notice this other road when we first got here."

Nancy looked at the small lane from which they had just emerged. There was a break in the stone wall surrounding River Arts, but it was overgrown with prickly raspberry bushes that half obscured the dirt tracks.

"It's not as if there were a neon sign marking it," she said. "The road is barely visible, thanks to these bushes. Anyway, whoever was here is long gone. We might as well go back to the sculpture garden and check the damage."

She and Bess circled back to the sculpture garden by way of the main entrance. Nancy shone her penlight on Rhoda's new sculpture, then grimaced when she saw a huge, splintered dent in one of the wooden spheres. One of the other geometric shapes—a hollow, wooden tube that hung like a chime from a metal rod—was bent and cracked where the sledgehammer had hit it.

"This is bad," Bess murmured.

"Well, now we know for sure that whoever spraypainted that threat on Rhoda's car really meant it," Nancy said. "This is the second attack today."

The strains of a song from *West Side Story* wafted across the air from the lawn near the house. "It's a good thing the sound is so loud," Nancy said. Moving slowly around Rhoda's sculpture, she beamed her penlight in every direction. "We'll be able to search for clues without the distraction of everyone running to see . . ."

Nancy's voice trailed off as the light glinted off something shiny in the grass near the base of the sculpture.

"What? Did you find something?" Bess was next

to her in an instant. Crouching, she watched with interest as Nancy picked up a slender silver-colored metal object.

"A pocketknife," Nancy said, turning it over in her hand.

"Do you think it could be Shane's?" Bess asked. "He was using a metal pocketknife in the kitchen this morning, remember? But"—she glanced up from the knife with perplexed eyes—"didn't we just decide Bruce Pennington was the person we saw here?"

Nancy closed her hand tightly around the knife and rose. "We need some explanations," she said, "starting with one from Shane."

She and Bess made their way back around the art studio building and up the sloping lawn to where the movie screen was set up. They stood to one side of the rows of chairs, scanning the faces that were turned toward the screen.

"There!" Bess whispered. She pointed to where Rosie sat, near the back. Shane filled the seat next to hers. Bess raised an eyebrow at Nancy, then walked to the very back row and slipped into a seat right behind Rosie and Shane.

"Excuse me," Nancy said, dropping onto the chair next to Bess. She tapped Shane on the shoulder.

"Hmm?" Shane murmured. He and Rosie turned toward Nancy at the same time.

"Sorry to interrupt the movie," Nancy whispered,

"but something just happened, and I need to talk to you about it." She went on to describe the damaged sculpture and the person she and Bess had seen.

As she spoke, Rosie's face filled with horror. "That's awful!" she said in a shocked whisper.

Shane listened in stony silence, his arms crossed over his chest.

"Actually, we found something we think belongs to you, Mr. Mallory," Bess said.

Nancy held out the metal pocketknife. Seeing it, Shane scowled but remained silent.

"Dad?" Rosie bit her lip. "Is that yours? Were you there?" she asked.

Shane didn't answer right away. Still scowling, he took the pocketknife from Nancy. His eyes flashed with anger as he shook the folded knife at Nancy and Bess.

"I don't owe you any explanations," he said in a steely voice. "You or anyone else!"

"Shh!" someone hissed from in front of them.

"Listen here." Shane lowered his voice to an angry whisper. "You leave Rosie and me alone, or you'll be sorry!"

With that, Shane turned away and leaned heavily against the chair back. Nancy felt awful when she saw the mix of confusion and doubt and shock in Rosie's eyes. Then Rosie, too, returned to the movie.

Bess opened her mouth to say something, but

Nancy held a finger to her lips. Standing up, she motioned for Bess to follow her. She didn't stop until they were out of Shane's hearing range, near the pillars outside the front door to the house.

"Did you hear that threat?" Bess whispered.

Nancy nodded. "We definitely have to tell Rhoda about this," she said. She let out a long breath. "This case has so many pieces that don't seem to fit together. I mean, the clues make it seem that both Shane and Bruce were in the sculpture garden tonight. Could they be working together? And what about Marco? He's been up to something weird."

As she spoke, Nancy looked for Marco's head. He and TJ had been sitting near the front earlier, and she saw that they were still there. "I don't see how he could have had anything to do with what just happened in the sculpture garden, but"—Nancy grinned at Bess as an idea came to her—"now's my chance to find out more about what he has been up to."

"Uh-oh. I know that look." Bess giggled. "It means you're about to get both of us mixed up in something sneaky."

"It takes a sneak to catch a sneak," Nancy replied. "If I'm going to prove Marco is up to no good, I'll have to be as wily as he is. All you have to do is stay with Marco and TJ. Make sure they don't go to their room until after I'm done searching it."

"No problem," Bess said with a broad grin. "Turning the charm on guys happens to be my specialty."

Nancy waited until she saw Bess sit down next to Marco. Then she went inside and hurried to the north wing of the house, where the students' rooms were. She wasn't sure which room was Marco's, but just about every room had a message board hanging outside the door. Nancy examined each one. When she reached the door right next to the room she and Bess shared, she finally found what she was looking for: two notes addressed to Marco scribbled on the message board.

"Yes!" she whispered. This had to be his room.

She looked carefully left and right, then took a deep breath, turned the doorknob, and opened the door a crack.

So far so good, she thought. The room was dark and silent. In one swift motion, Nancy slipped inside and closed the door behind her.

"Now what?" she wondered aloud.

Once she was inside, Nancy saw that Marco and TJ's room wasn't totally dark. The window over-looked the lawn where *West Side Story* was being shown, and the shade was up. Flickering lights from the screen played over the room's two beds, dressers, and the jumble of items that covered the floor and desks.

Taking a deep breath, she started toward the closest bed. "I might as well start—"

Nancy blinked, surprised, as her ankle hit a wire that was stretched taut just above the floor.

Click.

"What the—"

She didn't have time to finish her thought. All of a sudden a blinding light flooded the room. Sirens blared, making Nancy freeze in her tracks.

She saw a network of strings that reached from the light switch and tape player to a wire that extended across the room, a few inches above the floor.

A trip wire! This can't be happening! her mind screamed.

But it was.

With a stab of panic, Nancy realized she was in plain sight of everyone watching the movie outside. Heads turned. People rose out of their chairs to see what was happening. Nancy groaned when she spotted Marco's spiky blond hair. His beady eyes were staring directly at her.

Great, she thought. Now Marco, and every other person out there, knows I sneaked in here.

7

Caught!

Nancy felt like a deer caught in the blinding head-lights of a car. The blaring sirens echoed off the walls, making it impossible to think. Shooting her hand out, Nancy slammed her forefinger down on the Stop button of the tape player.

Finally! she thought as the shrieking noise stopped.

She drew a relieved breath, but it caught in her throat when she saw Marco running toward the building. His voice carried clearly through the open window as he called, "Hey! What are you doing up there?"

Nancy gulped as Marco and TJ made a beeline for the front door. How am I going to get out of this one?

Then she saw Bess angle in front of Marco and TJ, shooting them an exaggerated smile. The three of them disappeared from Nancy's sight, and she heard them coming down the hall a moment later.

"Nancy is such a goof!" Bess was saying. "I can't believe she got our room mixed up with yours."

Yes! thought Nancy. Leave it to Bess to come up with the perfect excuse.

As TJ, Marco, and Bess opened the door, she held up her hands, trying to look apologetic. "Sorry, guys," Nancy said, playing along with what Bess had said. "Our room is right next door. I guess I got confused."

She couldn't tell whether or not Marco believed her. His expression was as irreverent as ever.

"Ha! She fell right into our trap," he said, giving TJ a high five.

Nancy blinked. He was right, she realized. She *had* been trapped. She'd been so taken by surprise that she hadn't thought about it until that moment.

"Why did you set up the trip wire?" she asked.

"I guess you could call it our own personal security system," TJ answered, shrugging.

Security? Nancy thought. Why did they need security? Was it because they had something to hide?

She looked around the room, taking in everything for the first time. Marco's black sports bag was on the floor, sitting half open amid a pile of clothes next to one of the beds.

Bess had spotted the bag, too, Nancy saw. She took

a step toward it, shooting another big smile toward Marco and TJ.

"If you ask me, you guys need a housekeeping system, not more security," Bess said.

Nancy saw immediately what Bess was up to. In just a moment she would able to see inside the bag.

Marco pushed past Bess swiftly. He shoved the bag far underneath his bed, then grabbed an armful of clothes and threw them into the air like confetti. "The messier the better," he said as the clothes rained down.

Nancy sighed. Marco was doing it again, acting as if everything were a big performance.

And she and Bess were no closer to finding out if threats and vandalism were a part of his act.

"Let me get this straight," Rhoda said Thursday morning. "You think Bruce Pennington did this?"

Using a wrench and pliers, Rhoda finished detaching the dented, splintered sphere from her sculpture. She handed it to Bess, who laid the piece on the ground next to the busted tube Nancy had already removed.

"It's possible," Nancy said. She stepped away from the sculpture and crouched next to her backpack, which lay in the grass. Inside was her notebook, with notes on everything they knew about the threats and vandalism so far.

"The candy wrapper is pretty strong evidence that

he's the one we chased to that back drive," Nancy went on, flipping the notebook open. "It also makes sense that he would know about the road since the estate belongs to his aunt."

She and Bess had told Rhoda about the damage to her sculpture the night before, but it had been so late that Rhoda decided to hold off inspecting the damage. After grabbing coffee and muffins from the breakfast buffet in the dining room, the three of them had lugged the toolbox to the sculpture garden. Students and teachers wound down paths and across the lawn on their way to classes and work sessions. Nancy was glad no one passed too close to the sculpture garden so that they could talk about the case.

"If Bruce wants to wreck River Arts, he's off to a good start," Rhoda said. She gave an angry shake of her head that sent her braids swinging. "The work crew won't finish cleaning and repairing the fire damage to the studios for a few days. In the meantime the art students are using whatever space they can find. And who knows when I'll be able to find the time to repair my sculpture?"

Rhoda let the pliers and wrench fall into the toolbox with a clunk. Planting her hands on the hips of the long batik dress she wore, she stood silently for a moment. Nancy saw her dark eyes move from the broken sculpture pieces to the art studio building just beyond the sculpture garden.

"What about Mrs. Pennington?" Bess asked, biting her lip. "You don't think she would actually cancel your lease, do you?"

"She's been understanding so far," Rhoda said. "But to tell you the truth, I'm a little afraid of what she might do if Bruce causes any more damage."

Nancy sat down on the grass, letting the sun warm her face. "We still can't be sure Bruce is the person we're after, especially when there's evidence pointing to other people," she said, running a finger down the list in her notebook. "Gemma was in the art studio building right before the fire yesterday. And Marco was definitely eavesdropping outside Mrs. Pennington's window."

"Besides, he's probably hiding something in that black bag he carries around," Bess observed.

Rhoda sat down next to Nancy and plucked a blade of grass. "I don't trust Gemma," Rhoda said slowly. "But Marco?" She frowned, twisting the grass between her fingers. "I hate to think he'd do something to hurt River Arts. He's rebellious, sure, but he's talented, too. Why would he wreck the place that's giving him the chance to learn with a fantastic professional actor like Craig Harrison?"

"Beats me," Nancy replied. "All I know is that he was nowhere to be found yesterday afternoon. I think it's possible that Bruce could have convinced him to set the fire." Taking a deep breath, she added,

"There's someone else we need to consider, too."

She exchanged a meaningful look with Bess, then told Rhoda about finding Shane's pocketknife. Rhoda held up a hand to stop her.

"I already told you, Shane's not involved," she said.

"How can you be so sure?" Bess asked.

"I know Shane. He's as upset about what's been going on here as I am," Rhoda said. "I want you to leave him alone."

Nancy wasn't certain she could make that promise, not when there was evidence that clearly implicated Shane. "Well," she said, choosing her words carefully, "do you have any idea why Shane has been acting so aloof? And why his knife was here?"

"I'm not going to demand explanations from Shane. That would be an insult to a good friend," Rhoda said. "Besides, I—"

"Rhoda!" a man's voice called from the direction of the art studios.

Nancy turned to see Craig Harrison striding toward them. His running shorts and T-shirt were stained with sweat, and his brown skin glistened. In his hands was a bulging manila envelope, which he waved in the air.

"I found this outside the estate entrance when I got back from my run," Craig said, dropping the envelope into Rhoda's lap. "I was going to leave it in your office, but then I saw you down here."

"Special delivery, eh?" Rhoda smiled up at Craig. "Thanks."

As Craig jogged back toward the house, she ripped open the envelope. Immediately the air was filled with a foul smell that made Nancy gag.

"Ugh!" said Bess, holding her nose. "What is it?"

Holding the envelope away from her, Rhoda spilled its contents onto the grass. A strip of newspaper fluttered out, amid a shower of shredded flowers.

"Roses?" Nancy said. She frowned and took a closer look. "They've been all hacked up!"

"What a stink," Rhoda said, grimacing.

Nancy picked up some of the petals and sniffed them, then shuddered. "Sulfur," she announced.

"Look at this!" Bess plucked the newspaper strip from the pile and held it out.

Nancy scowled when she saw the newspaper article. It was the one they had seen about River Arts in the *River Heights News* the day before.

"My picture!" Rhoda whispered. Her eyes were wide with horror as she stared at the clipping.

Rhoda's face in the newspaper photograph had been crossed out with black ink. The pen strokes were so savage that they had worn a hole right through the paper. Below the photograph, in the same black ink, someone had scrawled a message: "I'LL MAKE SURE YOU *NEVER* SMELL THE ROSES."

8

Foul Play

"Not again." Rhoda groaned.

Nancy felt her stomach bottom out. "The threats are definitely getting worse," she said.

"I'll say." Bess glanced uncertainly at Rhoda. "This threat sounds personal—against you, not River Arts."

Rhoda's mouth clamped into a tight line as she swept the flowers back into the envelope and folded it shut. Then she stood up and faced Nancy and Bess.

"We need to get to the bottom of this," she said, her eyes flashing with determination. "I want you two to follow every lead and find out who's trying to destroy me."

"We'll start with Gemma Vance and Bruce Pennington," Nancy said.

Rhoda nodded. "Gemma runs an art school for kids in downtown River Heights," she said. "I'm not sure where Bruce has his office, but I'm sure we can find the address in the phone book. I've got one in my office. You two go ahead. I'll finish up here."

"We're on it!" Nancy said. She tossed her notebook into her backpack and jumped to her feet.

Rhoda's office was at the rear of the house, overlooking the patio. Books and files filled the shelves and were piled across a wide oak desk. Sculptures, drawings, and paintings covered the walls and filled every open nook in the room.

"Here," Bess said, plucking a thick phone directory from the shelf behind Rhoda's desk. She flipped through the pages and scrawled two addresses on a notepad. Ripping the sheet from the pad, she shoved it into her shorts pocket. "Got 'em. Come on, let's go!"

Twenty minutes later Nancy pulled her Mustang to a stop in front of a strip of stores in downtown River Heights. There, between a clothing boutique and a jewelry store, was a wide storefront window with a neon sign that read, Vance Art Studios.

"Uh-oh," Bess said. She pointed to a Closed sign that hung in the windowed door. "What do we do now?"

Nancy gazed through the window and caught sight of Gemma's short, sleek black hair and curvy figure. Gemma stood in front of an easel at the back of the studio, working on a painting.

"She's in there," Nancy said. Slinging her backpack over her shoulder, she knocked at the door until Gemma came to open it.

"Sorry, we're closed," Gemma said, blocking the doorway with her body. "I've got twenty kids arriving for art camp on Monday, plus a gallery show to put up today. . . ." She trailed off, looking back and forth between Nancy and Bess. "Do I know you from somewhere?" she asked.

"We were at River Arts when you came to teach landscape painting yesterday," Nancy replied. Seeing Gemma's face tighten, she quickly said, "We felt really bad about how Ms. Benton treated you. We were psyched to take the class."

Nancy made up her story as she went along, hoping Gemma would warm up to them.

"That's right," Bess said. "The class sounded so interesting, we decided to come here to find out more about it."

Gemma's expression softened immediately. "Well, I guess I could spare a few minutes," she said, stepping aside to let Nancy and Bess in.

The art studio consisted of one wide, spacious room. Shelves and cabinets ran along the back wall, but Nancy noticed there were plenty of supplies that hadn't been put away. Cardboard boxes filled with canvas, paints, brushes, and other materials were scattered across the floor. Easels and stools stood against the wall.

If they could just look through the things, Nancy thought, she and Bess might find evidence linking Gemma to the threats or vandalism at River Arts. Catching Bess's eye, Nancy nodded at the boxes. Then she stepped over to the easel at the back of the room, where Gemma had been working.

"Is this painting yours?" Nancy asked.

"Why, yes," Gemma said, joining her.

Perfect, Nancy thought. Gemma didn't seem to notice that Bess had stayed behind and was strolling among the boxes. Now, if I can just keep Gemma occupied . . .

"It's going to be part of an exhibit of my paintings at a local gallery," Gemma told her. "I'm putting the finishing touches on it before I install the show this afternoon."

"Mmm." Nancy cocked her head and looked at the painting. She didn't think the view—of a hillside with some houses and church spires sticking up among the trees—was anything special. Still, she didn't want to insult Gemma.

"There must be a real art to teaching landscape painting," she said, changing the subject. "Were you going to use a particular method at River Arts yesterday?"

"It *is* an art, believe me—not that Rhoda Benton will ever give me credit for it." Gemma shook her head and let out an angry breath. "Local artists should help one another out. I don't know who Rhoda thinks she is, trying to keep me out of River Arts. I'm the best teacher she'll—"

"Whoa . . ." Bess's surprised voice came from behind Nancy and Gemma.

Gemma whirled around. Seeing Bess bent over a cardboard box near the front window, she frowned. Her sandals tapped on the linoleum floor as she walked over to Bess. "What are you doing?" she demanded.

"Looking at these," Bess said. As she straightened up, Nancy saw two red paisley bandannas dangling from each hand. "Bandannas just like these were used to start that fire in the art studios at River Arts yesterday."

"Wait a minute." Gemma tapped her sandal on the floor, and her eyes flicked from Nancy to Bess. "What kind of stunt are you two pulling?"

Think fast, Drew, Nancy told herself. She decided to be as direct as she could without blowing their cover.

"We're Rhoda Benton's interns," Nancy said. "We were at the art studios after the fire when Rhoda found out that someone set the fire using red bandannas."

"So you decided to snoop around here so you could pin it on me?" Gemma snorted and eyed Nancy even more closely. "What did you say your name was?"

"Nancy Drew," Nancy answered, "and this is Bess Marvin."

"Drew? You're not related to Carson Drew, are you?" Gemma asked.

"The River Heights Man of the Year?" Bess piped up. "He's Nancy's dad."

Gemma's eyes flickered over Nancy a moment longer. Then she grabbed the red bandannas from Bess. "These things aren't exactly rare, you know. You can buy them in a dozen different places in town," she said. "Not that it's any of your business, but these are for a collage project I'm planning for the kids in my camp."

Her explanation sounded reasonable. But Nancy couldn't ignore the fact that Gemma had been in the studio at River Arts just before the fire.

"Someone's been threatening Rhoda," Nancy said. "And last night someone damaged one of her sculptures."

She watched Gemma closely for a reaction. If Gemma had had anything to do with damaging the sculpture, she showed no sign of it.

"Poor Rhoda," Gemma said, returning the bandannas to their box. "Excuse me if I don't cry, but she's got plenty of people helping her these days. Rhoda has made it crystal clear that I'm not going to be a part of River Arts. Why should I care what happens to her?" She strode to the door and held it open. "I think you'd better leave now," she said.

Nancy and Bess didn't say anything more until they were back in Nancy's car.

"Wow," Bess said, combing her fingers through her hair, "Gemma sure is jealous of Rhoda."

"Yes, but jealous enough to risk going to jail by setting fires and damaging Rhoda's property?" Nancy asked. After tucking her pack into the backseat, she started the car and backed out of the parking spot. "Anyway, Gemma's right about the bandannas. Just because she has the same ones doesn't mean she started the fire. We need more solid evidence."

"That stinks," Bess observed. She reached into her shorts pocket and pulled out the note paper she'd brought from Rhoda's office. "Well," she said, tapping a finger at the second address on the sheet, "maybe we'll have better luck at Bruce Pennington's office."

"So what's our plan?" Bess asked Nancy fifteen minutes later.

They had just pulled up in front of an office building that sat behind the stores and restaurants of the renovated waterfront. "I wish I knew," Nancy said. "If Bruce recognizes us, there's no way he'll ever let us look around his office, or—"

"Look! Isn't that him?" Bess whispered.

She sank lower in the car seat, nodding toward the entrance of the office building. Bruce Pennington, wearing a polo shirt and khaki pants, had just emerged through the rotating doors.

"Perfect!" Nancy said as he turned the corner, whistling. She grabbed her backpack and opened the car door. "Let's move."

A few minutes later they stepped out of the elevator on the fourth floor of the building. The door in front of them had a frosted glass panel in it, with "BP Ventures" painted on it in black letters. Nancy paused with her hand on the door handle.

"See if you can distract whoever's in here long enough for me to sneak into Bruce's office and look around," she whispered.

Bess gave her the thumbs-up, then followed as Nancy opened the door and entered BP Ventures.

The office was fairly small, Nancy saw. Beyond the reception desk there was a carpeted hallway with a few doors leading off it. Nancy glimpsed a coffee machine, a table and chairs, and the corner of a refrigerator through one door. Through another, she saw a desk covered with blueprints.

Good, she thought. Other than the receptionist, a woman with chin-length brown hair and glasses, there didn't seem to be anyone around.

"May I help you?" the receptionist asked, smiling at Nancy and Bess across the counter.

"We'd like to see Mr. Pennington, please," Nancy said.

When the woman told them he wasn't in, Nancy tried to look surprised. "Perhaps we could wait for him in his office?" she said.

The receptionist replied. "Mr. Pennington won't be back for some time. Could I ask what this is in reference—"

"Aiieee!" Bess suddenly fell onto the smooth carpeting, clutching her ankle. "My ankle!" she exclaimed, twisting her face into a pained expression. "I tripped on something, and . . . I think I've sprained it."

"Oh no! Let me see." The receptionist jumped up from behind her desk. As she bent over Bess's ankle, she didn't notice Bess wink at Nancy.

"If I could just get some ice," Bess said, with a weak smile that looked totally convincing.

The receptionist nodded. "Of course. We've got ice in our break area at the back of the office," she said. "Here, let me help you."

Great! thought Nancy. Now, if I can just sneak into Bruce's office . . .

"I'll use my cell phone to call the doctor," she fibbed.

She pulled her cell phone from her backpack. As the receptionist helped Bess down the hall, Nancy slipped quietly into the office.

Quick, she thought. Shoving the phone back in her pack, she closed the door behind her and inspected the room. There's not much time.

She saw a candy-filled bowl on the desk. Each candy had a bright red wrapper marked with a distinctive and familiar white zigzag.

That clinches it, Nancy thought. Bruce *had* to be the person she and Bess had chased the night before. Still, she knew she had to find more concrete proof linking him to the vandalism.

She set her pack on the floor next to the desk and quickly pushed aside the blueprints. Beneath them were half a dozen phone memos from someone named Justin Laroche, each with the word urgent written at the bottom. The name meant nothing to Nancy. She filed it away in her mind, then began opening desk drawers.

"Pens, paper clips, drafting supplies," she murmured, "building codes . . ."

She let out a sigh of frustration. She felt as if she were looking for a needle in a haystack, and the seconds were ticking away fast. Bess wouldn't be able to keep the receptionist busy forever.

Nancy opened a file drawer and glanced at dozens of labels. "Greerson Offices" . . . "High Street Warehouse Conversion" . . .

"Bingo!" she whispered as she spotted a file near the front labeled "Riverfront Condos."

She plucked the file from the drawer and flipped through the thick wad of papers. Many of them were from someone named . . .

"Justin Laroche," Nancy said.

From what she could tell, Laroche was a key financial backer for some of Bruce Pennington's projects. As Nancy skimmed the papers, she saw mention of both the Riverfront condo project and the high-rise office building going up down the street from where her father worked. Her head swam with phrases snatched from the letters and memos: "Pleased to have your assurance that you are moving ahead on the riverfront development of your aunt's property . . . Office high-rise riskier, but acceptable as part of a package that includes riverfront condos. . . ."

In more recent communications, Laroche was more critical: "Disappointed in your failure to secure property for riverfront condos . . . Without the condo project to guarantee a profit, I must reconsider your entire development plan. . . . I cannot justify continued funding of your risky high-rise venture. . . ."

Nancy drummed her fingers against the most recent letter, dated just a few weeks earlier. In it Laroche wrote that Bruce had broken their agreement when he failed to secure the condo development deal. Consequently, Laroche was going to pull his funding out of the office high-rise, which he thought was too costly.

"Ouch," Nancy said, wincing at the harsh words.

No wonder Bruce had seemed so stressed out. If Laroche withdrew his funding, Bruce would be in serious financial trouble.

Her mind raced as she replaced the file and slid the drawer shut. Talk about a strong motive for wanting to convince his aunt to back out of her contract with River Arts, she thought, as she grabbed her pack and headed for the door. Wait till Bess hears about—

"Miss Carlyle!" A deep voice boomed from the hallway right outside the office.

Bruce Pennington! Nancy froze halfway to the door.

"I'd like a cup of coffee, please," Bruce said.

In the next second Nancy heard the doorknob to the office rattle.

He was about to catch her red-handed.

9

A Close Call

Nancy's eyes flew over the desk, filing cabinet, shelves, and—

The closet!

She'd been so busy going through the desk she hadn't even seen the sliding doors to the closet. One door was half open, and Nancy dived through it. She landed on some boots with a soft thud just as the door opened.

Please, *please,* don't come over here, she begged silently.

She heard footsteps on the carpet, then the squeak of upholstery as Bruce sat down at his desk. Nancy sighed in relief. She couldn't see him from where she sat in the closet, but she heard a series of electronic bleeps as he punched a number into his phone.

"Justin?" Bruce said after a moment.

Nancy jolted to attention. The bulky boots on the closet floor dug into her legs, but she didn't dare move. She hardly breathed, for fear that Bruce would hear her.

"Bruce here. Listen, I just wanted to let you know it's all settled. The riverfront condo development project north of town is moving forward."

Nancy frowned into the dim, stuffy air inside the closet. How could the condo project move forward? Unless . . . Could Marianna Pennington have decided to back out of her agreement with River Arts and let Bruce go ahead with the condo project?

"I know we've hit snags before." Bruce's voice cut into her thoughts. "Trust me, this time our problems are over. . . . What? . . . Yes, you have my personal guarantee. My lawyers are drawing up the contract right now and—"

"Mr. Pennington!" Bess cried from down the hall. "Can you help me, please? It's important!"

I'll say it's important, Nancy thought. I've got to get out of here!

For a moment she was afraid Bruce wouldn't take the bait. Then she heard him say into the phone, "I'll call when the deal is final. . . . Yes, goodbye."

He clicked off, and Nancy heard his chair shift. She held her breath, watching through the half-opened closet door. A second later she got a glimpse of the back of his khaki slacks and white shirt as he left the room.

Now! Nancy pushed herself off the bulky boots and out of the closet and tiptoed to the door. She peeked around the doorframe just far enough to see the break room.

Bruce stood with his back to Nancy. He was bent over Bess's ankle, and Nancy could see Bess's face over his shoulder. Miss Carlyle's voice came from inside the room, saying, "Where's your friend?"

Nancy caught Bess's eye, gave the thumbs-up sign, and hurried back to the reception area. The last thing she heard before she slipped out of the office was Bess saying, "My friend must have gone to bring the car right to the front door. Thanks for all the help. My ankle is feeling a lot better now."

Nancy hit the elevator button, and soon she was safely on her way to the lobby.

"That was close," Bess said when she met Nancy outside a few minutes later. "Sorry I didn't have time to distract Bruce *before* he trapped you in his office. I practically died when I saw him go in there!"

"It was worth almost getting caught. You're not going to believe what I found out," Nancy said.

As they walked toward the car, she told Bess about the phone call she'd overheard and about what she'd read in Bruce's file on the riverfront condominium project.

"That proves it!" Bess said. "He *must* be causing all the damage at River Arts. I guess he doesn't mind wrecking Rhoda's dream *or* his aunt's estate—as long as the condo deal goes through so he doesn't lose his financial backing."

"Bruce sure has motive, but we still don't have proof that he's the vandal," Nancy said.

Bess shook her head in disgust. "We can't let him get away with it."

"We won't," Nancy said firmly. "We're going to keep a close watch on Bruce whenever he's at River Arts from now on. But first . . ." She pulled her cell phone from her backpack and turned it on.

"Who are you calling?" Bess asked.

"Dad," Nancy told her. "It's already Thursday, and the dinner honoring him is on Saturday night. I just want to check in to let him know how the case is going."

Her father's line rang just twice before his secretary answered. "Carson Drew's office," she said.

"Hi, Ms. Hanson. It's me, Nancy," Nancy said. "Is the River Heights Man of the Year in?"

"You just missed him, Nancy. He's out to lunch, but I'm glad you called," she said. "I was hoping you could do me a favor."

"Something for Dad?" Nancy asked, curious.

"You guessed it. I'd like to make a scrapbook of all the articles that have been written about him in the

River Heights News over the years," Ms. Hanson said. "I want to give it to him at the dinner Saturday. The trouble is, we're busy preparing for a case, and I haven't been able to get over to the newspaper office yet—"

"Say no more," Nancy said into her cell phone. "Bess and I are near the *News* office now. We'll pick up copies from the archives and get them to you before Saturday."

"Thanks. You're an angel," Ms. Hanson said.

After saying goodbye, Nancy clicked off and then started the Mustang. "We've got one more errand while we're in town," she said to Bess. "Next stop the *River Heights News.*"

"Make that *two* more stops," said Bess. "Let's get pizza first and then go to the newspaper office. I'm starved!"

"Look at all these articles!" Bess said two and a half hours later, as she and Nancy drove back to River Arts.

"Fifty-seven of them, to be precise." Nancy laughed and glanced at the pile of photocopied newspaper articles that lay in Bess's lap. "It's a good thing they have a computerized search engine for back issues of the *River Heights News.* Otherwise we'd have been looking through microfilm all day."

"No kidding. Some of these articles are a dozen

years old," Bess remarked. A warm wind blew over the top of the windshield, sending her blond hair whipping behind her. She kept a firm grip on the papers, leafing through them while Nancy drove. "Like this one."

Glancing rapidly, Nancy spotted a headline that read, "Local Lawyer Claims Workfare Works."

"That must be about the workfare program that gave Rhoda her start as an artist," Nancy said.

"Yup," Bess said. "This was written not long after the program was started."

Moving her finger down the edge of the article, Bess read, "'Criminal lawyer Carson Drew, who worked with Congressman James Sweeney to pass the bill, points to the successes of the workfare program in the six short months it has been in operation.'"

Nancy sat back and listened. It felt good to push aside thoughts of vandalism and threats—even for just a few minutes.

"Listen to this, Nan. Your dad talks about Rhoda!" Bess said. She leaned over the photocopy and kept reading. "'Mr. Drew referred to recent workfare graduate Rhoda Benton as a case in point. In an interview with this reporter, Mr. Drew said, "Workfare has provided Ms. Benton with valuable skills and a vocation she cares about. Clearly, she is a reformed person and she no longer represents a threat to society."'"

Bess turned to Nancy and grinned. "Doesn't it feel good to know your dad had a part in helping Rhoda change her life?" she said.

"Her, and lots of other people, too," Nancy said. "I'm so proud of Dad."

"According to this, not everyone was as crazy about workfare as your dad and Rhoda, though," Bess said, going back to the article.

"No?"

Bess pointed to a paragraph about halfway down the article. "This mentions members of some citizens' group that thought workfare was too easy on criminals. Then there were other people who criticized it because it didn't help enough people."

"I guess you can't please everyone," Nancy said, shaking her head. "I think Dad did a great job of—"

"Oh my gosh!" Bess gasped, interrupting Nancy. "I can't believe I didn't notice this before."

"What?" Nancy glanced sideways as Bess jabbed a finger at the bottom of the article.

"The reporter interviewed a small-time criminal who didn't qualify for workfare because of a previous record," Bess answered. "Guess who it was?"

Her eyes flashed with such intense excitement that Nancy almost couldn't stand the suspense. "Tell me!" she demanded.

"It was Shane Mallory," Bess said.

Nancy drove in silence, letting the information

sink in. Up ahead she saw the stone arch of the River Arts entrance appear.

"Listen to this quote," Bess said. She took a deep breath, then read, "'Mr. Mallory expressed bitterness at the workfare program, saying, "Rhoda Benton is no different from me. Why does she get a second chance, and I don't? It's not fair."'"

"Wow," Nancy said. She turned off the road, drove through the entrance to River Arts, and headed for the parking lot. "Rhoda thinks Shane is a friend, but he sure sounds angry in that quote. I wonder . . ."

As soon as she pulled to a stop, Nancy took her cell phone and dialed her father's number. This time he was there. Nancy smiled when she heard his deep voice say, "How's my favorite daughter?"

"I'm your *only* daughter, remember?" she told him. "Anyway, this is a serious call. I think you might know something about a person who could be behind the threats and vandalism at River Arts."

She went on to tell him about her suspicions of Shane. "We think he might be jealous that workfare gave Rhoda a leg up when he didn't qualify. Do you remember anything about him?"

"Mallory, eh?" Carson repeated. "Oh, yes, now I remember. He was one of the people Rhoda used to hang out with back in her troubled years. As far as I know, he never did get his act together. He's been in and out of jail for years—mostly for small crimes.

Petty theft, breaking and entering, vandalism . . ."

"Vandalism?" Nancy grimaced. "You never heard anything about his being a chef on a cruise ship?"

"Afraid not. As far as I know, he's always lived in River Heights." Carson gave a small laugh before saying, "There aren't too many cruise ships around here, in case you haven't noticed."

"Thanks for the info, Dad," Nancy told him. After saying goodbye, she clicked off.

"Shane lied to Rosie about being a chef on a cruise ship," Nancy told Bess. She quickly relayed the information her dad had given her.

"He obviously hid his jail record from Rosie," Bess said. "But . . . well, it's been a long time since that article. Why would he wait until now to get back at Rhoda?"

Nancy got out of the car and shut the door behind her. "I'm not sure, but I think we'd better tell Rhoda about this. Maybe she can help us to . . ."

Her voice trailed off as she noticed a bright blue sedan parked next to the Mustang. "Check it out," she said.

"Huh?" Dropping the photocopies on her seat, Bess tumbled out of the passenger side and hurried toward Nancy.

"The paint. It's scratched down this whole side of the car." Nancy arched an eyebrow, running her fingers along a scratch on the door. "The scratches are fresh, too. As if someone had recently driven this car down a narrow road overgrown with—"

"Raspberry bushes!" Bess said.

Nancy knelt next to the fender and peered into the wheel well. "It looks as if something is wedged in here."

She reached in and tugged on something stiff and prickly. She gritted her teeth and pulled out a handful of bent, exhaust-stained raspberry vines.

"I knew it!" she cried.

"So," Bess said, gaping at the tendrils, "this car belongs to the person who vandalized Rhoda's sculpture!"

10

Telltale Vines

"We have to find out who this car belongs to," Nancy said.

"Shane?" Bess said.

Nancy tried the two doors on the driver's side, but they were locked. "Maybe," she answered. She circled to the other side of the car, peering through the windows. "I don't remember seeing it before, though. And . . ."

Just then she saw paintings stacked across the backseat. The one closest to her featured a green hillside dotted with church spires and houses.

"We saw that painting this morning, at Vance Art Studios," Nancy said.

"You mean, this car belongs to Gemma Vance?" Bess bent close to the window and stared through it at the paintings. "Didn't she say she was putting up an exhibition of her paintings in a gallery in town this afternoon? What's she doing here?"

As Nancy mulled the questions over, she heard footsteps and heated conversation coming from nearby. She saw Gemma Vance emerge from the woods, followed closely by the River Arts painting teacher, Susan Gimble. To judge by the angry scowl on Susan's face, an argument was brewing between them.

"Don't be ridiculous," Gemma was saying. "Of course I can hang my paintings in the River Arts Gallery. I'm having a exhibition there, after all."

Nancy caught the surprised glint in Bess's eyes. "You mean, *this* is where she's having her gallery show?" Bess whispered.

Nancy shrugged, still listening to Gemma and Susan.

"You can't exhibit in our gallery!" Susan said heatedly. She followed on Gemma's heels as Gemma circled Nancy's Mustang to the blue car. "For one thing, no one gave you permission. For another, there's already a full exhibit of paintings on display, done by River Arts students and teachers."

Gemma dismissed Susan with a wave of her hand. "I've started taking those down to make room for my own paintings," she said.

"What!" Susan stopped next to the blue car, letting

her breath out in an angry stream. "You're impossible!"

Gemma stopped when she saw Nancy and Bess next to her car. "You again?" she said, her eyes flashing with annoyance. "What are you . . ."

She didn't even bother to finish her own question. "Oh, never mind. I'm too busy to deal with a couple of teen troublemakers," she muttered.

With that, Gemma unlocked her car, grabbed an armful of paintings, and headed back into the woods the way she had come. Susan stayed with Gemma, continuing to dispute her. "If you think for a second that you're going to get away with this," Susan said angrily, "you are *sooo* wrong."

"Let's go with them," Nancy said to Bess. "I want to keep an eye on Gemma and ask her about these." She held up the handful of thorny raspberry vines she had found wedged behind the wheel of Gemma's car.

They hurried through the woods and emerged into the sunshine behind the house a minute later. Gemma and Susan were so busy arguing that they didn't seem to notice the two men fixing the slate tiles Marco and TJ had broken on the patio. Moving quickly, Nancy and Bess followed the two women around the side of the house.

Nancy paused as they rounded the corner to the front of the house. The wide lawn stretched left, past the house and fountain to the art studios and sculpture garden beyond. Straight ahead, the grass sloped gently down toward the river. A wide path wound into the oaks, maples, and linden trees that edged the grass to the right. Nancy thought she remembered that it led to the dance studios and drama center. Just beyond the path a new-looking white stucco building was nestled into the trees. Gemma and Susan were heading for it.

"Isn't that the gallery?" Bess asked.

"Right," Nancy said, still following the women. "Let's hope they stop arguing long enough for us to—"

"Nancy! Bess!" a guy's voice called out.

Nancy caught sight of Marco and TJ standing next to the fountain.

"Come here for a second," Marco called. "I want to ask you something."

"Not those two," Bess said, rolling her eyes. "Keep your eyes opened, Nan. Who knows what kind of booby trap they've set up for us this time?"

"Don't worry," Nancy said. She glanced at the River Arts Gallery. Gemma and Susan were just disappearing inside. Nancy guessed they would be there for at least a few minutes, so she started toward Marco and TJ.

Nancy noticed that TJ, wearing shorts and a Hawaiian shirt, had his video camera trained on her and Bess. Marco stood next to him in baggy cutoffs and a sleeveless T-shirt. Both guys watched her and Bess with eyes that were filled with . . . Nancy couldn't tell whether it was amusement or mischief.

"What's up?" she asked, stopping next to the fountain.

"Well, we were just noticing something," Marco said. "For interns, you two don't seem to do very much. I mean, I haven't seen you here all day long."

"Did it ever occur to you that maybe Rhoda sent us on an errand *outside* River Arts?" Nancy said in what she hoped was a confident voice. The last thing she and Bess needed was to have one of their suspects snooping on them.

"Doing what?" TJ shifted his video camera to aim it at the raspberry branches in Nancy's hand. "Picking berries?"

Bess shot an annoyed glare at the video camera TJ still aimed at her and Nancy. "Don't you ever put that thing down?" she asked.

"Sure, sometimes." TJ lowered his camera, and Nancy saw that an impish smile had spread across his face. "Like when Marco and I have something important to do."

What was he getting at? Nancy wondered.

"Like now, for instance," Marco said. "I mean, if you two are going to goof off, you might as well learn how to do it right. And TJ and I are just the ones to teach you."

With a taunting grin, he reached out and gave Nancy's shoulder a shove.

"Hey!" Nancy cried out, stumbling backward. She felt the backs of her knees push up against the stone rim of the fountain, throwing her off balance. Her feet flew out from under her, and she toppled backward, hitting the shallow water in the fountain with a splash.

"Oooh!" As Nancy floundered, a second splash sent more water showering over her. The next thing she knew, Bess was beside her in the fountain.

"This means war!" Bess cried, her wet hair plastered to her face.

"You said it," Nancy growled. She reached out to grab Marco's arm and pulled him in.

He hit the water, then sent a huge spray of water back at Nancy with his hands. "*This* is the way to goof off," he said, laughing.

TJ didn't even wait to be pulled in. After laying his video camera on the grass a safe distance away, he jumped in. Before long the fountain was filled with students drawn by the noise of the water fight.

Nancy had to admit it was fun to let loose. There were people everywhere and a constant spray of water flying around them. Someone had made water balloons and was lobbing them from an upstairs window of the house.

"Isn't this great?" Bess said as she dodged a water balloon.

Nancy nodded, then stopped as her gaze fell on the white stucco gallery next to the trees. "Oh my gosh, I totally forgot about Gemma," she said.

"Me, too." Bess wiped the water from her face. "What if she leaves before we have a chance to talk to her?"

Nancy sat on the rim of the fountain, squeezing water from the bottom of her T-shirt. The raspberry vines were gone—lost among the splashing water fighters. "I can't believe we let Marco drag us into this," she groaned. "I mean, we are on a case and—"

"Where *is* Marco anyway?" Bess asked.

Nancy scanned the crowd of squealing, splashing students. "He's not here," she said. "I wonder where—"

"Aiiiieee!"

An earsplitting shriek rang into the air. The terrified, bone-chilling sound sent a shiver up and down Nancy's spine.

"What was that?" Bess asked, in the uneasy silence that fell over the fountain.

"Something's wrong," Nancy said. "Something's very, very wrong."

11

A Scream of Terror

Nancy was out of the fountain in a flash. Hands on hips, she scanned the woods to the right of the house. "That scream sounded as if it came from there," she said.

"Isn't that where the dance studios are?" Bess asked.

Nancy didn't wait for an answer. She took off across the lawn, heading for a path she saw winding into the trees. Water squished from her soggy sneakers a clothes. Every step was a struggle.

"Why did I let Marco distract me with that water fight?" she muttered.

Nancy made herself move faster. As she raced into the woods, she glimpsed a wooden building through the trees ahead.

"Wait up!" she heard Bess call from behind. Glancing over her shoulder, Nancy saw Bess amid a knot of dripping wet students. They all looked worried—and with good reason, Nancy thought. That scream still echoed in her mind.

Moments later she burst into a clearing. Right in front of her was a large wooden stable that had been converted to dance studios. Several skylights had been built into the roof. The old stable door was flanked by two new doors that had been cut into the weathered boards on either side. The doors were marked Studio A, Studio B, and Studio C. Seeing the door to Studio C ajar, Nancy raced toward it.

"Hello?" she yelled as she went through the door. "Is anyone—" She stopped short. "Oh no!"

Rosie stood at the center of the dance studio, wearing a leotard, warm-up pants, and sneakers. Her face was deathly white. She stared in horror at the mirrors that ran the length of one wall.

Every single mirrored panel had been smashed.

The smooth hardwood floor was covered with sharp silver shards that glinted in the afternoon light. As Nancy hurried to Rosie, her reflection in the smashed mirrors was broken and distorted. "Rosie, are you all right?" Nancy asked.

"I, uh . . ." Rosie shook herself as Bess and the others burst through the door. "I'm fine," she said. "Why is everyone all wet?"

"Water fight. No big deal," Bess said. She looked around with wide, shocked eyes. "What happened *here*?"

Rosie shrugged. "I came to warm up before my work session with Marc Flanders. He's my dance teacher," she said. "But when I got here . . ." She took a deep breath and let it out slowly. "Who would do something like this?" she asked in a whisper.

"You can bet we're going to try to find out," Nancy told her. "You didn't see or hear anyone when you got here?"

Rosie shook her head. "No, but there's a back door," she said. "I guess someone could have gone out that way when I came in the front."

There was a doorway at the other end of the studio, Nancy saw. It opened on to a hallway that ran along the back of the three studios. Nancy noticed doors to the bathrooms and, beyond them, a back door. She hurried to the end of the hall and pushed the door open.

"It's just woods," Rosie said, coming up alongside her. She pointed to a path that went into the trees. "That leads to the parking lot."

"So whoever smashed the mirrors could have made a pretty quick getaway," Nancy observed. She stepped outside and took in every inch of the area around the back door. "Hey—what's this?"

She moved quickly to the spot where the path

snaked into the woods. There, lying in the ivy that edged the path, was a hammer. "Whoever smashed the mirrors must have used this," she said, picking it up.

Rosie started toward the path determinedly. "Maybe we can catch the person!" she said.

"We can try," Nancy replied. She had already taken a few running steps when she heard the back door to the dance studio bang open.

"Hey, wait for me!" Bess called, and ran up to Nancy and Rosie.

"The others are going to find Rhoda and your dad, Rosie," Bess said. Nodding at the hammer in Nancy's hand, she asked, "The weapon?"

"Yup," Nancy said, nodding. "Now, if we can only find the culprit."

The three of them raced along the wooded path, brushing past branches and shrubs. Nancy was getting used to the clammy, heavy feeling of her wet clothes and sneakers. Alert for any sound or movement, she kept her eyes focused ahead. When they reached the parking lot a minute later, she whipped her head around quickly, then let out a sigh.

"No one here but us," she said.

"The parking lot is minus one car, too, in case you haven't noticed," Bess said. Arching an eyebrow at Nancy, she walked over to the empty space next to Nancy's Mustang.

"Gemma's," Nancy said. The bright blue sedan was gone. That means Gemma is definitely a suspect, she thought.

"Gemma Vance?" Rosie stared blankly from Nancy to Bess. "Why would she smash the mirrors in the dance studio?"

"That's something we haven't figured out yet," Nancy replied. "All we know is that she's pretty steamed about not getting hired at River Arts and—"

"Hey, Nancy, you left your backpack in the car," Bess said.

She was leaning over the open top of the Mustang. She pulled the backpack from the floor in the back and held it up.

"I totally forgot about it," Nancy said. "I guess we left it here when we went to look at Gemma's car—" She broke off, staring at the empty passenger seat. "Wait a second. Didn't you leave the newspaper articles we copied for Dad, too?"

"Definitely. We were in such a hurry to follow Gemma I didn't think to pick them up." Bess scowled. "They're gone."

"Gone?" Rosie echoed. "You mean, someone took them? Why would anyone do that?"

Nancy glanced uneasily at Rosie. A possible answer to the last question popped into her head. But she was sure it was an answer Rosie wouldn't be happy with. What if Shane had taken the articles to make sure no one at River Arts found out about his criminal past?

"Um, Rosie," Nancy said, choosing her words carefully, "do you have any idea what your dad has been doing today?"

"No," Rosie answered. "What does that have to do with—" She broke off suddenly. "You think *he* took your articles?"

"It's possible," Nancy answered.

Rosie stood quietly for a moment, then shook her head angrily. "No way. I can't believe you guys," she said. "First you accuse Dad of smashing Rhoda's sculpture. Now this! What would my dad want with your stupid newspaper articles anyway?"

"Maybe we should tell her," Bess said.

"Tell me what!" Rosie demanded.

Nancy took a deep breath and said, "We're pretty sure your dad was never a chef on a cruise ship."

Rosie's eyes clouded over, but Nancy made herself go on. She told Rosie about Shane's criminal record and about the angry comment he had made about Rhoda in the old *News* article about workfare.

"I—I don't believe it!" Rosie recoiled from Nancy and Bess, as if she were suddenly allergic to them. "You're lying," she said.

"It's the truth, Rosie," Bess told her. "Your dad sounded pretty bitter about Rhoda's getting a second chance when he didn't. That's why we think—"

"What's going on here?" a deep voice boomed.

Nancy wheeled around to see Shane stride into the graveled lot from the wooded path that led from the dance studios. To judge by the hot red spots on his cheeks, Nancy guessed he had overheard them.

"I-is it true, Dad?" Rosie said. "You've been . . . in jail?"

Shane's face fell. For a long moment he just stood there. Then he nodded and said, "Rosie, I—"

"How could you lie to me?" Rosie burst out. He took a step toward her, but she said, "Leave me alone!" Blinking back tears, she ran past him and disappeared into the woods.

"Should we go to her?" Bess said, gazing worriedly after Rosie.

"You leave Rosie alone!" Shane yelled.

There was a hard edge to his voice, but Nancy faced him squarely and said, "She deserved to know the truth, Mr. Mallory."

"I'm not going to let you ruin everything for me," Shane said, biting out the words. "This is the last time I'm going to warn you. Leave me and Rosie be!"

For one awful second Nancy was afraid he would hit her. His chest heaved, and his face grew purple. Then he whirled about and stormed off in the direction Rosie had taken.

"Rhoda?" Nancy called as she and Bess stopped outside the door to Rhoda's office a few minutes later.

"Not in?" Bess said when no one answered.

Nancy bit back a sigh. So much had happened. She and Bess really needed to talk it all over with Rhoda. But it looked as if they would have to wait.

Nancy turned to leave, then brightened when she saw Rhoda walking toward them down the hall. "Just the person we were looking for," she said.

"I was inspecting the damage to the dance studio," Rhoda said. "Our custodial crew has already started cleaning up the mess. Thank goodness we can have new mirrors installed tomorrow." She led the way into her office, then slumped into the chair behind her desk. "When is it going to end?" she asked.

"Well, we've got a lot of leads," Nancy told her as she and Bess sat in two chairs that faced Rhoda's desk. "The trouble is, so far the evidence points to a few *different* people."

She and Bess told Rhoda about their visits to Vance Art Studios and BP Ventures. Rhoda listened quietly, nodding occasionally. When she heard about the conversation Nancy had overheard between Bruce and his financial backer, Rhoda straightened up, instantly more alert.

"How can Bruce go ahead with his condo plan?" she said. "Marianna hasn't said a word to me about canceling our lease." She drummed her fingers against the desktop. "He *must* be the one who's behind all this vandalism."

"No one saw him here today," Nancy told her, "but he could have convinced someone to help him."

"Someone like Marco," Bess remarked. "I mean, doesn't it seem a strange coincidence that he side-tracked us right before the mirrors in the dance studio were smashed? And the way he disappeared . . ."

Rhoda nodded. Nancy could see that she was convinced Bruce was the culprit.

"Gemma was here, too," Nancy said, thinking it all out as she spoke, "*and* she was here just before the fire yesterday."

"Not to mention that we found those raspberry vines caught behind her car wheel," Bess said.

"Susan told me about the stunt Gemma pulled at the gallery," Rhoda said. "She finally persuaded Gemma to take her paintings and leave."

"*Before* the mirrors were smashed?" Nancy asked.

"Yes," Rhoda answered. "Susan wasn't sure of the exact time, but she said it was definitely before she heard Rosie scream."

That meant Gemma could have been responsible, thought Nancy. The gallery wasn't far from the dance studios. Also, the path through the woods to the parking lot would have given Gemma a chance to get away without being detected.

"Bess and I still wonder about Shane, too," Nancy said. Before Rhoda could object, she hurried to say, "We know about his criminal record."

"That's all in the past," Rhoda said.

"Yes, but—" Nancy exchanged quick glances with Bess. They then told Rhoda about the photocopied articles' being taken from Nancy's car—and about their run-in with Shane in the parking lot.

"I know you think he's a friend, but what if he's been feeling resentful toward you all these years?" Bess asked when they had finished.

Rhoda sighed. "If Shane lied about his past to Rosie, it must be because he wanted to make a good impression. Period," she said.

"What about the quote in the article?" Nancy asked. "Shane said it wasn't fair that you qualified for workfare when he didn't. He was definitely resentful."

"That was, what, twelve years ago?" Rhoda shook her head again. "I just don't buy it. I mean, sure, Shane has had a hard life, but I don't think he holds my success against me." She swiveled her chair around and gazed through the French doors at the patio outside. "Anyway, River Arts has given him a chance to spend time with Rosie. Why would he do something to ruin that?"

Nancy wasn't sure of the answer to that question. All she was sure of was that the evidence against Shane was mounting. She unzipped her backpack and reached inside for her notebook.

Nancy was puzzled when she saw a folded sheet of

paper on top of the notebook. She pulled it out and unfolded it. "It's a note," she said.

Leaning forward in her chair, she held the paper out so Rhoda and Bess could read the words scrawled across it in block letters: "I CAN HELP YOU. MEET ME AT THE GAZEBO TONIGHT AT MIDNIGHT."

"Someone must have slipped this into my pack when I left it in my car," she said.

"Shane?" Bess asked. Her forehead creased into worried lines as she stared at the note. "I don't know, Nan. What if it's a trap?"

"I can't let you put yourself into danger," Rhoda said.

"It could be a trap," Nancy said. She curved her mouth into a sly smile. "But what if we come up with a plan to trap the trapper?"

At five minutes to midnight Nancy stepped out the front door of the River Arts house. She moved speedily from the yellow glow of the lamps outside the door into the velvety darkness.

Lanterns sparkled in the night, marking the paths that led to the art and dance studios, the River Arts Gallery, and the drama center. Nancy moved past them, toward the shadowy darkness that shrouded the cliff overlooking the river.

As she moved down the gentle slope toward the cliff, she made out the jet black silhouette of the gazebo ahead. Goose bumps popped out on her arms and legs. She wasn't sure who might be watching her.

"Keep cool," Nancy told herself. "Whatever you do, don't give Bess and Rhoda away."

She glanced at the woods to the right of the gazebo. She couldn't see Rhoda and Bess among the tangle of shadows, but she knew they were there. If anyone *did* try to hurt Nancy, they would be there immediately to help turn the tables on the attacker.

Taking a deep breath, Nancy stepped into the gazebo. She pulled her penlight from her jeans pocket and shone it on her watch. It was midnight.

"Okay," she murmured, her eyes and ears alert. "Where are you?"

She leaned against the ivy-covered stone wall against which the gazebo had been built. The rushing waters of the Muskoka were far below. All Nancy saw was ivy that faded to a swirling, gurgling blackness. Wind whipped up from the river and blew through the leafy tendrils. It would have been pleasant if it hadn't been for—

All of a sudden Nancy heard a muffled cry in the woods to her right. Then she heard Bess shouting, "Hey, stop!"

Nancy whirled around and stared hard at the shadows. She heard thrashing leaves and branches snapping beneath heavy footsteps. Flashlight beams blinked on. That had to be Bess and Rhoda chasing someone!

The beams bobbed so wildly that Nancy couldn't see much of anything. She took a step, then paused when she heard something else: footsteps coming up behind her.

"What—"

Before Nancy could turn to see who it was, two hands shoved roughly against her shoulder blades. She hit the stone wall and flipped over its top.

"Noooo!" she cried.

Then she felt herself falling toward the rushing river far below.

12

A Close Call

Nancy threw her arms out, trying to grab something, *anything*. Cold, stark terror stabbed at her as the night air rushed past her.

All at once her hand closed around a thick knot of ivy. She winced as her body jerked to a halt. Her arm felt as if it would pull right out of its socket. "Come on, Drew. You can do it," she told herself, reaching up and clamping on with her other hand.

Gritting her teeth, she pressed her feet against the ivy-covered wall and angled her body out in a V. She tried not to think about the long drop below. Slowly, steadily, she moved one hand above the other. Her feet kept slipping on the ivy, but she hung on with every ounce of her strength. Finally, after what seemed like an eternity, she was able to hook a leg over the top of the wall and heave herself into the gazebo.

Nancy collapsed on to the gazebo floor, then jolted to sitting again when she heard shouts and the sounds of people scrambling through the woods.

"Oh my gosh!" Nancy gasped, jumping to her feet. "Rhoda and Bess could be in trouble!"

She raced after the sounds into the woods. At first all she saw were flashlight beams flickering behind a thick mass of bushes ahead. Within moments the voices came closer. As Nancy angled around the thick bushes, she kept her eyes focused ahead.

"Ooomph!"

Nancy gasped as she ran headlong into . . .

"Marco!"

He stumbled back a few steps, blinking and shaking his head. "What the—"

Nancy spotted the black sports bag Marco had dropped. "What's in there?" she demanded.

Marco glared at her, then snatched up the bag. "None of your business."

They both turned at the sound of footsteps. A moment later Rhoda and Bess appeared, their faces lit up by the flashlights they carried. Rhoda shone her light on Marco, making his hair glow almost white in the night.

"I thought I recognized that hair," she said, leaning forward to catch her breath. "Show us what's in the bag, Marco."

Marco squinted into the light, then crossed his arms over his chest. "You want to see, *you* open it," he said.

Nancy couldn't believe how defiant he was, even when he'd been caught. She dropped to her knees, yanked on the zipper, and opened the bag so everyone could see inside.

"Money?" Bess said.

Nancy could hardly believe her eyes. Wads of bills were rolled and packed into the bag. "There must be hundreds of dollars here," she said.

Leaning closer, she spotted something metallic among the bills. She reached in and pulled out a video camera and some spotlights. Beneath them were a straw hat and a pair of flowered gardening gloves.

"You stole Mrs. Pennington's gardening things?" Bess said.

"And isn't this TJ's?" Nancy asked, holding up the video camera.

Rhoda's feet crunched on some dried leaves as she stepped over to Marco's bag and picked it up by the straps. "Stealing from people at River Arts is bad enough," she said, fixing Marco with a angry gaze, "but taking money to vandalize the arts colony . . . How dare you?"

Nancy would have expected Marco to look guilty, at the very least. Instead he just threw back his head and laughed. "You think *I'm* the big bad vandal who's been terrorizing River Arts? What a riot!"

"Are you trying to tell us you *weren't* paid to set that fire and smash the mirrors in the dance studio?" Bess asked.

Marco opened his mouth to respond. Before he could, a forceful voice spoke up from behind them: "Marco has done nothing wrong."

Out of the shadows stepped Marianna Pennington, wearing slacks and a light jacket.

"Mrs. Pennington!" Rhoda exclaimed. "What are you doing here?"

Mrs. Pennington walked over to Marco. A smile spread across her face, and she said, "Marco invited me to be part of his performance piece, and I accepted. We were on our way to the theater-in-the-round when you two"—she nodded at Bess and Rhoda— "decided to chase us."

Nancy had a hard time making sense of what she was hearing. "You're working on a performance project?" she asked. "In the middle of the night?"

Marco rolled his eyes. "Not that I should have to explain myself," he said, "but I wanted to video an interview with Mrs. Pennington, one I can play in the background during my performance piece."

"Why Mrs. Pennington?" Bess wanted to know, and Nancy understood why. Marco's story *did* sound far-fetched.

"She's a pretty cool lady," Marco replied, shrugging. "I found that out after TJ and I broke those tiles on the patio yesterday."

"Marco came to apologize, and we got to talking about his project," Mrs. Pennington told them. "Oh, by the way, if you check those *wads* of money, you'll find that they're all fake. But good enough for the camera, I understand." She looked as though she was about to burst out laughing.

"Why didn't you say something about this piece of theater before, Marco?" Rhoda asked.

Marco shrugged, holding up his hands. "What kind of impact would it have?" he said. "Mrs. Pennington and I have been rehearsing in secret."

"So *that's* what you were up to the afternoon the fire was set," Nancy said.

"And today, when the mirrors in the dance studio were smashed," Bess said.

"You got it," Marco said. "That's why I wanted to film the video of Mrs. Pennington at night, too. I figured a night video would have more atmosphere. And who would be around to see us?" He kicked at a branch. "How were we supposed to know you guys would have a commando squad waiting to chase us down?"

Nancy glanced back and forth between Marco and Mrs. Pennington. She had heard enough to convince her that Marco was telling the truth.

But if he's not the person who's vandalizing River Arts, she thought, then who is?

"It's too bad you showed up when you did," Nancy said. "Bess and Rhoda were so busy chasing you that the person who lured me out here got away—after trying to kill me."

"What!" Rhoda, Bess, Marco, and Mrs. Pennington all cried.

Nancy told them about being pushed over the cliff from the gazebo.

"Oh my gosh!" Bess said. "You could have died!"

"You didn't see who pushed you?" Rhoda asked.

"Whoever it was pushed me from behind," Nancy said. "We still don't know who the vandal is or what his or her next move will be."

"I definitely need my coffee this morning," Nancy said, filling her mug from the urn that was set up on the breakfast buffet.

Bess yawned, then filled her mug, and added milk and two spoonsful of sugar. "No kidding," she replied. "We didn't go to sleep until after two in the morning, and it's only eight now. That's not much of a beauty rest."

Nancy couldn't help laughing. "I guess not. But you know what they say: The early bird catches the clues. I want to go over the scenes of all the vandalism again. Maybe we missed something."

Bess grabbed a cranberry muffin from a platter, then paused. "Speaking of missing something," she said, lowering her voice, "Rosie looks as if she missed even more sleep than we did."

Rosie had just walked into the dining room. There were dark circles under her eyes, and her black curls looked as if they hadn't been combed. Seeing Nancy and Bess, she stopped short.

"Um, hi, Rosie," Nancy said. "I'm sorry if—"

"Save it," Rosie said. She held her shoulders straight as she walked over to the buffet table, but she looked as if she might cry. She sat on the other side of the room and wouldn't even look at Nancy and Bess.

"I feel awful," Bess whispered as she and Nancy left the house, fifteen minutes later. "If we *do* find any more clues, for Rosie's sake I hope they prove Shane is innocent."

"Let's start with the art studios," Nancy said, heading down the sloping lawn toward the building. "The repair work is mostly done, but we might be able to—"

She stopped and cocked her head to one side. She thought she heard the faint, steady droning of an engine through the trees. "Hear that?" she asked, snatching Bess's arm. "It's a car, and it's driving down that back lane!"

"The one where we chased the person who damaged Rhoda's sculpture?" Bess peered toward the trees, but Nancy pulled her the other way.

"Come on," Nancy said, sprinting toward the parking lot. "This time we're not going to let whoever it is get away!"

They were breathless by the time they reached the lot, but Nancy didn't slow her pace. As soon as Bess and she were strapped in, Nancy started her Mustang and shifted into Drive. Flying gravel was reflected in the rearview mirror as they screeched out the driveway and headed toward the River Arts entrance arch.

"We've got to get there before the person pulls out of the lane." Nancy banged on the steering wheel, as if that would make the car go faster.

Seconds later she drove beneath the arch. She made herself slow to a stop before turning onto the road outside River Arts.

"Nancy, look!" Bess pointed up ahead, where the hood of a red vehicle was just nosing out of the narrow lane.

"Oh, no, you don't," Nancy said.

She hit the gas, and the Mustang shot forward. By the time the red SUV pulled completely out of the lane, Nancy and Bess were close enough to see who was behind the wheel.

"It's Bruce Pennington!" Bess said.

At that moment Bruce glanced at the Mustang.

His eyes met Nancy's, and his expression darkened.

"Mr. Pennington, stop!" Nancy called.

Bruce threw one last glare at Nancy and Bess, then turned away. In the next instant his SUV shot away from them. With tires screeching, he took off down the road at top speed.

13

The Chase Is On!

"He's getting away!" Bess cried.

"Not if I can help it," Nancy said.

She pressed harder on the gas, and the Mustang shot forward. Up ahead, Bruce's SUV was a red splotch that shone brightly in the morning sun. Nancy kept her eyes on it as the Mustang sped after it.

"Come on," she said, inching her speed up to the limit.

She heard Bess's gasp as the SUV disappeared around a tree-lined curve ahead of them. A moment later the Mustang flew around the curve and—

"He's turning off!" Bess cried.

Half a football field ahead, the SUV sped right through a red light and screeched into a right turn.

"Talk about dangerous," Bess muttered. "It's a

good thing there's not much traffic this early."

"He's heading for the bridge!" Nancy said.

The traffic light blinked green a split second before Nancy reached it. She yanked the wheel right and took the turn as fast as she safely could. Ahead of them, the cables of the bridge stretched across the Muskoka in graceful scallops. Sunlight glared off the SUV roof as it shot onto the metal span some seventy-five yards ahead.

"We'll never catch up with him!" Bess moaned.

"Never say never," Nancy replied. She gripped the wheel tighter, as if somehow that might make the car go faster. Wind whipped over the top of the windshield, sending her hair flying out behind her. The Mustang inched closer to the SUV, but when Bruce reached the other end of the bridge, he was still fifty yards ahead of them.

"Oh my gosh!" Bess said, gripping her seat. "Doesn't he see that red light?"

A traffic light at the far side of the bridge had just turned red. Bruce's SUV shot toward it without slowing down in the least. Nancy's heart leaped into her throat when she saw the line of cars on the road that crossed the bridge road. A white hatchback began inching across the intersection—directly in the path of Bruce's SUV.

"Oh no!" Nancy exclaimed. "He's going to hit someone."

The next few seconds passed in a blur of squealing

brakes and blaring horns. Nancy was sure there would be a crash. At the last second the SUV swerved sharply around the white hatchback, tipping onto two wheels.

Nancy wasn't sure how it happened, but somehow the white car got safely across the intersection. By the time Nancy reached the traffic light, Bruce's SUV had run off the road onto the shoulder. It spun around in a full circle before jerking to a stop against the guardrail.

"I've got you now," Nancy muttered. She pulled her car off the road and stopped directly in front of the SUV, blocking Bruce's path. In no time she and Bess were out of the car and next to the SUV.

"Are you all right, Mr. Pennington?" Bess asked, leaning close to the open window.

Bruce sat behind the wheel, dazed. He nodded, then scowled at Bess and Nancy. "This is all your fault!" he growled.

"*Our* fault?" Bess took a step back and set her hands on her hips. "*You're* the one who's been vandalizing River Arts, not us," she said hotly.

"Look, you're wasting my time with these crazy accusations and chasing me," Bruce said, clearly annoyed.

"Well, why did you run?" Nancy asked.

"Wouldn't you if someone were tailing you?" he answered. He raked a hand through his short brown hair, then brought it down with a thud on the dashboard—right next to some discarded red-and-white candy wrappers.

"Someone damaged Rhoda's sculpture on Wednesday night," Nancy said, making no move to get out of the way. "Whoever it was made a getaway down that lane you just came out of. Afterward Bess and I found candy wrappers just like these."

She pointed to the wrappers, but Bruce barely glanced at them. "You're way out of line, accusing me," he said. "Why would I waste my time with Rhoda Benton's sculptures?"

"I happen to know that Justin Laroche threatened to pull his financial backing if you didn't pull together the deal for the riverfront condos," Nancy replied.

That got Bruce's attention. His mouth fell open. "How did you—"

Without going into details, Nancy said, "I heard you on the phone with him when Bess was in your office yesterday." She saw Bruce's eyes flicker with recognition as he turned to Bess. But Nancy didn't give him a second to say anything.

"I can't believe you actually set fires and smashed mirrors and stuff, just so your aunt would back out of her contract with River Arts," she said, shaking her head in disgust. "That is *so* low."

Bruce's face grew red. "I don't have time for this," he muttered. "You want to know why I've been coming to River Arts?" He picked up a rolled-up blue-print from the passenger seat, slid off the rubber band, and unrolled it. "I *have* been working on a riverfront condo development project," he said. "But *not* on my aunt's property. For your information, the property I'm developing is across the river!"

Bruce jabbed a finger at the blueprint. Nancy spotted an architectural drawing of both sides of the Muskoka River. Sure enough, the highlighted area was directly across the river from River Arts.

"But," she said, trying to make sense of what he'd just told her, "what were you doing in that overgrown lane behind River Arts?"

"Taking photographs." Bruce pointed to a camera case that also lay on the passenger seat. "The view from my aunt's property is perfect. Rhoda and I don't exactly get along, so I decided to use the back road, where I wouldn't bother her and she wouldn't bother me."

As he spoke, Bruce rerolled the blueprint and carefully slid the rubber band around it. "I took one set of photos on Tuesday afternoon," he told them. "They didn't come out very well, so I came back today to take some more."

"Tuesday afternoon?" Bess echoed. She leaned against the door of the SUV, fixing Bruce with a doubting stare. "We chased you from the sculpture garden on *Wednesday* night."

"I don't know who you chased," Bruce said, "but it

wasn't me. My lawyer was in the office with me until after ten that night, working out the details of the condo plan. Just ask my secretary if you don't believe me." He checked his watch and frowned. "Look, I really have to get to this meeting. Justin Laroche doesn't like to be kept waiting."

Nancy bit her lip, thinking. Bruce's alibi would be easy to check out. Besides, her instinct told her he was telling the truth. "Thanks for explaining everything, Mr. Pennington," she said.

"And good luck with the condo deal," Bess told him.

They got back into Nancy's car. She pulled it out of the way of Bruce's SUV and watched him drive off.

"Well, we're back to square one," Bess said. "We still don't know who the vandal is."

"Mmm." Nancy felt the warm breeze on her face as she turned around and headed back across the bridge toward River Arts. "At least we have a pretty good idea of who it *isn't*," she said. "With Marco and Bruce out of the running as suspects, that leaves just Gemma and Shane."

"We did find those raspberry bush branches stuck behind the wheel of Gemma's car," Bess said, "and she was around River Arts when the fire was set and when the mirrors in the dance studio were smashed."

Gemma had acted suspiciously, thought Nancy. Still, she wasn't convinced Gemma was the person they were after. "I don't know," Nancy said. "Arson, vandalism . . . whoever did all that stuff even tried to kill me. It doesn't make sense to me that Gemma would do all that just because Rhoda didn't hire her to teach at River Arts."

"You don't think she has a strong enough motive?" Bess asked. "What about Shane?"

"I keep wondering about him," Nancy replied. "I know Rhoda trusts Shane. But for her own safety, I think we'd better find out more about him."

Nancy was cautious as she and Bess approached the River Arts kitchen a short while later. After their last run-in she didn't expect Shane to cooperate with them. Still, she thought, I'm not about to let his attitude stop us from finding out whether he's behind the threats and vandalism.

"Good." Nancy let out a sigh of relief when she peeked through the kitchen door and found the room empty. "He's not here."

"What are we looking for?" Bess asked, coming into the kitchen behind Nancy.

Nancy walked slowly through the room, observing the shiny counters, cabinets, shelves, and appliances. "I'm not sure," she answered. "Anything that connects Shane to the threats or vandalism. Magazines that have letters cut out of them, red spray paint, shards of mirror that might have gotten caught in his clothes and then dropped off later . . ."

She walked slowly past a hanging basket of garlic and onions, then ran her finger along a shelfful of bowls, cups, saucers, and plates. The room was clean and tidy. Nancy didn't see anything that didn't belong or that seemed suspicious.

"Nancy!" Bess's urgent voice made Nancy wheel around.

Bess was bent close to a shelf filled with cookbooks. As Nancy hurried over, Bess straightened up, holding up a thick wad of photocopies.

"So Shane took them," Nancy said.

Bess nodded, trying to smooth the folded, wrinkled sheets. "They were stuffed in behind the shelf," she said. "Shouldn't we tell Rhoda?"

"Definitely," Nancy said.

"Where *is* Shane anyway?" she asked.

Bess glanced out the kitchen window. "You don't think—"

"He's planning another attack? Not if I can help it," Nancy said. "You go find Rhoda. I'll look for Shane. If he's up to no good, maybe it's not too late to stop him!"

Nancy ran from the kitchen, clutching the photocopied articles in her hand, then wound her way to the front door. As soon as she was outside, she checked in every direction.

"Where *are* you?" she murmured to herself.

For the next twenty minutes, she went from build-ing to building, checking the gallery, the dance stu-dios, the drama center, and the theater-in-the-round. She found no sign of Shane—or of any damage. By the time she got to the art studios, she was breathless and sweaty.

"Nancy!" Susan Gimble looked up in alarm from the sinks, where she and Stu were washing paint-brushes. "Is everything all right?"

"Have you seen Shane?" Nancy asked.

They shook their heads. "Not since breakfast," Stu said. "Why are you—"

Nancy couldn't stick around for the rest of his ques-tion. She ran back out the door. "I'll explain later!" she called over her shoulder.

She raced toward the sculpture garden, keeping her eyes alert for Shane. The sculpture garden, too, appeared to be empty. Nancy stopped to catch her breath, her eyes still absorbing everything around her.

"Hmm, what's that?" Nancy wondered aloud. Using the newspaper articles to shade her eyes from the sun, she stared into the woods beyond the sculpture garden. Some weathered wooden panels were barely visible among the trees. They blended in so well that she hadn't noticed them before.

Nancy jogged closer. As she entered the woods, her sneakers crunched on leaves and branches. The cooler air felt soft on her skin. The wooden structure, some twenty feet in, had no windows and was small—about eight feet by ten feet, Nancy guessed.

Looks like some kind of shed, she thought. She stepped toward the metal door set into one wall, then froze about five feet away when she heard something.

Nancy stood absolutely silent, then jumped when she heard it again: the scuffle of feet inside the shed and the scrape of something metallic.

Someone was in there!

Her heart started beating like crazy. Moving as silently as she could, she made her way to the door.

Here goes, she thought. Taking a deep breath, she threw the door open and stepped inside.

"Who's there?" she asked.

There was no answer.

At first all Nancy saw was a circle of light that shone through the open door. Shelves lined the walls and were crammed into the center of the room, fading into blackness as they stretched farther inside the shed. Someone was inside, Nancy knew it. But in the shadowy darkness she couldn't see the person.

Slowly she took one step, then another. The sharp scent of turpentine was in the air. She squinted at the cans and bottles that filled the shelves: paints, turpentine, other solvents. There was a small arsenal of flammable material.

Nancy blinked, stepping deeper into the shed.

Her eyes were adjusting to the dark. The black shadows began to resolve into cans, boxes, and—

Just then she heard a shoe scrape against the concrete floor right next to her.

The next thing she knew, something hard had struck the back of her head.

Everything went black.

14

Shane's Story

"Ohhh," Nancy groaned, "my head."

The sound of her own voice floated in the darkness around her, as if in a dream. Nancy was dimly aware of a throbbing at the back of her head and of something cold and hard beneath her. Slowly she opened her eyes, then gasped.

"Shane!" she cried, wincing at the sharp pain that shot through her head.

She was lying on the concrete floor of the shed, she realized, with the photocopies scattered around her. As Shane moved toward her, his body blocked her way to the door. His taut, unreadable face loomed over her, making Nancy shiver.

"No!" She scrambled backward, sending papers skidding across the floor. She reached wildly with her hands, looking for something she could use to defend herself.

"Go easy, now," Shane said. "Are you all right?"

His concerned, gentle tone made Nancy blink, surprised. What kind of game was he playing?

"Your head's bleeding some," Shane told her. He removed his apron, folded it into a square, and handed to her. "Whoever knocked you out really meant business."

Nancy tried to fight off the woozy, cottony feeling inside her head. "Are you trying to say"—she touched the apron to the back of her head and felt a swollen lump. Sure enough, when she looked at the apron, there was a small spot of blood on it—"you're *not* the person who knocked me out?"

"You're finally figuring it out," Shane said with a sober nod. "I'm on your side, Nancy. If you weren't so set on my being a criminal, you might have realized you're not the only one trying to catch the person who's out to destroy River Arts."

His voice still held an angry note, but his eyes held such concern that Nancy found herself believing him. "But how— What are you doing here?"

"I've been keeping an eye out for trouble ever since Rhoda told me about the threat she found spray-painted on her van," Shane said. "Whenever I have the time, I walk around checking for anything that could be a target."

He reached out a hand, and Nancy let him help her to her feet. "Is that what you were doing Wednesday night, when I saw you sneaking toward the art studios?" she asked.

Shane nodded. "I figured it couldn't hurt to check for clues that you might have overlooked," he said. "I was inside the studio when I heard that racket in the sculpture garden. Then you and Bess took off after the person like a couple of rockets, so I—"

"Decided to check out the sculpture garden," Nancy said. She thought it out, filling in the blanks. "I guess you dropped your knife when you were there, huh?"

"That's right," Shane said. "Boy, was I steamed when you started demanding explanations. There I was, trying to catch the person who's after River Arts, and you acted as if I were the troublemaker."

"You have to admit you looked guilty," Nancy said. "Why didn't you just tell us what you were really doing?"

Shane stared moodily down at the floor, then bent down and began sweeping the scattered photocopied articles into a pile on the floor. "You don't know what it's like to have a criminal record," he said gruffly. "People hold it against you." He glanced sharply at her. "You did."

He was right, Nancy realized. "I'm sorry," she said. She knelt to pick up the articles. "Is that why you lied to Rosie?" she asked. "Because you didn't want *her* to hold your past record against you?"

Shane reached out to collect the last few scattered sheets before answering. "I was afraid she wouldn't come if she knew the truth, that she wouldn't want to get to know me," he said. "That's why I took these from you, too." Shane shuffled the sheets into a neater pile, then handed them to Nancy. "Of course, that plan backfired when you told Rosie about my record."

Nancy opened her mouth to explain, but Shane cut her off. "I know, I know. She deserved to know the truth. I realize that now," he said. "I told Rosie everything this morning after breakfast. At least now she knows why I've been sneaking off."

Nancy didn't hear the rest of what Shane said. She blinked, staring at the top photocopy in her hand. The stories were a dozen years old. Nancy recognized the article Bess had read the day before, under the headline "Local Lawyer Claims Workfare Works." But the article that now grabbed her attention was farther down the page.

"Is Workfare Soft on Criminals?" read the headline. "One Citizen Says Yes."

Nancy couldn't stop staring at the grainy photograph beneath the headline. A dark-haired young woman stood in front of two paintings that had been slashed to shreds. There was something familiar about the woman's curvy figure. Then Nancy read the caption beneath the photograph.

"Gemma Vance," she said.

"Huh?" Shane looked at her as if she had spoken in some completely incomprehensible code language.

"How could I not have noticed it before?" Nancy said. "This is a picture of Gemma!"

She held the photocopied page in the light of the doorway, so Shane could read the caption beneath the photograph: "Artist Gemma Vance in front of two of her vandalized paintings. Although police have made no arrests, Ms. Vance claims the hoodlums responsible are 'the very same people who are being channeled into the workfare program. 'If you ask me,' said Ms. Vance, 'workfare shows outright favoritism to criminals, while honest people like me are victims.'"

Shane looked up at Nancy and let out a whistle. "I remember now. There was some kind of incident with a young artist showing paintings in a gallery for the first time," he said, tapping the photocopy with his forefinger. "Some troublemakers broke into the place and slashed a bunch of paintings. I remember that the artist blamed it on workfare. But until this moment"—Shane glanced at the photo again and shook his head in amazement—"I never realized it was Gemma Vance."

"Gemma went a lot further than just blaming workfare," Nancy said, skimming the article at lightning speed. She pointed to the third paragraph. "She actually gave the name of the person she thought slashed her paintings. Someone who participated in workfare program."

"Rhoda?" Shane asked.

Nancy nodded. "Listen to this." She read, "'Rhoda Benton should be in jail for ruining my paintings,'" said Ms. Vance. "'Instead, she gets extra training, thanks to workfare. I'm the victim here. I lost a year's work, and what do I get? A big fat nothing.'"

"Rhoda didn't have anything to do with it," Shane said, scowling. "I know that for a fact because the guy who did slash the paintings bragged about it to me afterward."

"Talk about motive," Nancy said. "Bess and I couldn't figure out what could make Gemma so resentful that she would go as far as setting fires and trying to hurt people. Now I know."

She turned to Shane, expecting him to say something. Instead he stood gaping at the shelf next to Nancy. "Uh-oh," he said.

"What?" Nancy asked. "What is it?"

Frowning darkly, Shane pointed at an empty section of the shelf. "That whole shelf was full yesterday," Shane said. "I'm sure of it."

"Full of what?" Nancy asked, trying to stifle the worry that rose up inside her. "Paint? Turpentine? Mineral spirits?"

"What difference does it make? It's all flammable,"

Shane said. He tapped on the inside wall of the shed, and a metallic ping echoed in the air. "That's why Rhoda lined the walls of this place with some kind of flame-resistant metal."

"Too bad she couldn't make the rest of River Arts flame-resistant, too," Nancy said. "Whoever knocked me out could be setting a fire right now!"

In the instant that Shane met her gaze, Nancy saw fear reflected in his eyes. Then he bolted for the door. "We've got to call the police," he said.

Nancy caught up to him quickly. As they pounded through the woods toward the sculpture garden, she clutched the photocopies in one hand. "Why didn't I bring my cell phone with me?" she groaned. She wished she had thought to take her backpack—with her cell phone and notebook inside—with her when she and Bess went to breakfast.

"There's a phone in the kitchen," Shane said. "I'll use that one."

"I'll warn Rhoda and Bess," said Nancy. "Let's meet by the fountain in five minutes and start a search. I don't think we can afford to wait for the police to get here."

Shane's answer was a curt nod. When they ran through the front door of the house a moment later, he made a beeline for the kitchen. Nancy went the other way, toward Rhoda's office. By the time she pushed through the office door, she was completely breathless.

"Rhoda! Bess!" she called.

Nancy skidded to a stop inside the door. She was surprised to see the drapes drawn. The room was so dim that Nancy didn't see Rhoda and Bess at first.

"There you are!" she said, spotting the tops of their heads, on the far side of Rhoda's desk. It looked as if they were sitting on the floor, though she couldn't imagine why.

She headed toward them. "Shane and I just figured out who's been trying to wreck River Arts," she said, without waiting for them to speak. "It's—"

Nancy gasped as she rounded the desk. She could see Bess and Rhoda clearly now, and what she saw made her heart skip a beat.

Red bandannas were tied around their mouths. Bandannas had also been used to bind their ankles and wrists.

"Oh my gosh!" Nancy cried. "Gemma's already been here."

Bess's eyes widened with fear as Nancy dropped down next to her. Bess flashed a terrified look behind Nancy, one that made alarms go off inside Nancy's head.

"Don't tell me—" She started to turn, then winced as two hands pushed her roughly to the floor. Before she could regain her balance, she felt her arms being twisted and tied together behind her back.

"That'll teach you to mess with me," said an angry voice.

Nancy pulled herself around. Gemma Vance was

bent over her, holding a red paisley bandanna. As she used it to tie Nancy's ankles together, she gave an ice-cold laugh that sent shivers down Nancy's spine.

"You're not going to get away with this," Nancy said.

"Oh no?" After grabbing another bandanna from her back pocket, Gemma began to wind it around Nancy's mouth. "I've got all three of you now," she said, "and I'm going to make you pay."

15

Trapped!

Nancy's gaze moved from Gemma's sneering face to the five cans of turpentine resting on the floor behind her. Fear pierced Nancy. She's going to burn this whole place up—with us inside! she thought.

"Gemma, wait!" Nancy said, twisting her head away from the red bandanna.

She wasn't sure why she said it—just that she had to find a way to distract Gemma. Surely, Shane would come here looking for them when they didn't show up at the fountain.

"What now?" Gemma looked at Nancy with annoyance, but at least she pulled the bandanna away from Nancy's face.

"You really had us fooled," Nancy said, trying to sound impressed. "That was clever, the way you used

141

the back lane to get into River Arts without anyone seeing you."

"It was, wasn't it?" Gemma said with a satisfied smirk. She sat back on her heels and addressed Rhoda. "The biggest mistake you ever made was failing to hire me at River Arts. After I got the letter of rejection, I made a point of getting to know every inch of this place so I could get back at you."

Rhoda's eyes widened, but with the gag in her mouth she couldn't say anything.

"You thought I was just pestering you about the job." Gemma's voice was filled with disdain. "You never had a clue to what I was really up to."

Nancy maneuvered herself to a sitting position, leaning against the wall next to a metal sculpture on the floor. "You didn't really care about teaching landscape painting the other day, did you?" she asked. "You just wanted to get everyone out of the art studios so you could set that fire."

"Bravo, Nancy." Gemma let the bandanna drop to the floor and picked up one of the turpentine cans, which she lifted in a toast to Nancy. Then she unscrewed the cap and began to pour the turpentine onto the shelf that lined one wall of Rhoda's office.

A sick feeling churned Nancy's stomach as the sharp smell of turpentine filled the air. She saw that Bess and Rhoda were watching Gemma. In Rhoda's eyes was an expression of horror—and confusion.

Nancy couldn't imagine how awful she must feel, sitting by helplessly while Gemma ruined everything she'd worked so hard for. Rhoda probably still didn't understand what Gemma's real motive was.

"I know about the exhibition of your paintings that was vandalized twelve years ago," Nancy said to Gemma. "You blame Rhoda for that, don't you?"

Gemma had started to reach for another can of turpentine, but she stopped and faced Rhoda. "You fooled the police with your reformed citizen act, but you never fooled me," she said, spitting out the words. "You ruined my paintings, and now I'm going to ruin you!"

Rhoda shook her head and strained against the bandannas around her wrists, as if to deny the accusation.

"Rhoda isn't the one who slashed your paintings," Nancy said. "I know that for a fact."

"Don't pull that with me," Gemma said with a sneer. She picked up another can of turpentine and poured it over the chairs next to Rhoda's desk. "Your days of special treatment are over, Rhoda."

"Special treatment?" Nancy repeated. "Is that what you thought workfare was?"

Gemma nodded emphatically. "Special treatment for criminals," she said. "Rhoda was a criminal, but she got training, a leg up in the art world." She emptied the can, then tossed it angrily to the floor. "I was a victim. My paintings were ruined! But did anyone help me? No, they were too busy making sure Rhoda Benton and other criminals like her were a success."

"No one gave Rhoda her success," Nancy said. "If she succeeded as an artist, it's because she worked hard for it. It's because she has talent!" She couldn't believe how distorted Gemma's reasoning was. "Workfare gave her a second chance, but what she did with it was up to her."

Nancy saw the grateful expression in Rhoda's eyes, but Gemma just muttered, "That's more than I got." She turned to Rhoda, her face expressing her outrage. "You owed me! After what you did to me, the least you could have done to make up for it was to hire me to be the painting teacher here."

"You must have felt betrayed when you didn't get the job," Nancy said. "That's why you sent Rhoda a threat in the mail and those stinky roses. You must have spray-painted her van, too. But—"

"What?" Gemma asked impatiently.

"Well, how did you know Rhoda would be visiting my dad?" Nancy asked.

"That was a stroke of luck," Gemma said with a sharp laugh. "I was downtown buying supplies for my art camp when I spotted her getting out of her van."

Nancy panicked when she saw Gemma pull a matchbook from her back pocket. Keep talking! she told herself.

"The night after the fire you parked in that back lane and sneaked through the woods to the sculpture garden," Nancy said. "You must have parked there again when you attacked me at the gazebo last night. We thought Shane was the one who left the note in my backpack, but it was you, wasn't it?"

Gemma smiled, playing with the matchbook. "Oh yes," she answered. "I saw the pack in the backseat of your car when I returned to the parking lot after—"

"After you smashed the mirrors in the dance studio?" Nancy said.

"Right again. You were getting to be a pain, with your nosy questions and snooping," Gemma said. "I guess I should have expected it from the daughter of Carson Drew. Workfare was *his* idea, and now he's even getting an award!"

She scowled, shaking her head. "Anyone who favors criminals over victims deserves to suffer," she said. "When I saw your pack, I figured I could get back at your father *and* get you off my back—for good."

Nancy shivered at Gemma's cold, calculating tone. "You must have been disappointed when your plan didn't work," she said.

"No matter," Gemma said, shrugging. "Maybe that plan didn't work, but today's will. Even your snooping around in that shed couldn't stop me. And I can get out of River Arts without anyone knowing I was ever here, thanks to that overgrown lane through the woods."

She was right, Nancy realized. The woods were right behind the house. It would be easy for Gemma to make her way to her car without being seen.

"Shane is calling the police right now," Nancy said. "He'll be here any minute, and so will the police."

"In that case . . ." Gemma bent to retrieve the bandanna she'd dropped on the floor, then quickly used it to gag Nancy. Nancy winced as Gemma tugged the bandanna tight and tied it at the nape of her neck.

All Nancy could do was watch in horror while Gemma pulled a match loose and struck it against the matchbook. Immediately an orange flame ballooned out.

For a brief moment Gemma watched the flame with an expression of sick pleasure. Then she tossed it onto the turpentine-soaked shelves.

Whoosh!

Nancy gasped as flames enveloped the entire wall of shelves.

"Ta-ta," Gemma said.

With that, she tucked the book of matches into her back pocket, slipped out onto the patio through the French doors, and disappeared into the woods.

16

A Race Against Time

Flames shot up from the shelves, crackling loudly as they reached for the ceiling. Following the trail of turpentine, the fire moved quickly. Already the room was filling with a dense, hot smoke that burned Nancy's nostrils.

She coughed into the fabric in her mouth, all the while struggling against the bandannas that bound her wrists and ankles. Rhoda and Bess were also coughing. Nancy caught the looks of desperate fear in their eyes as they watched the flames spread to Rhoda's desk.

Then Nancy's eyes fell on the three cans of turpentine that were still full. They sat on the floor near the desk.

No! Nancy's mind screamed. When the flames hit them, those cans were sure to explode!

She yanked hard against the bandanna around her wrists. If only she could get a little leeway, she was sure she could twist her hands free.

She winced as something sharp struck her back, ripping through her shirt.

Rhoda's sculpture! Sweat streamed down Nancy's face, and the dense smoke stung her eyes, making it hard to see. Still, Nancy could feel a sharp metal edge on the sculpture. She began rubbing the bandanna against it.

There were flames all over, roaring louder every second. The blistering smoke seemed to suck the oxygen from the air, making Nancy feel light-headed. Her body shook with her coughing, but she didn't stop rubbing the bandanna against the metal edge.

"Glrrbbk!" Bess's shout came out as an incomprehensible gurgle, but her terrified eyes told Nancy all she needed to know. They gaped at the roaring flames that danced around the three full cans of turpentine.

It wouldn't be long before the cans would blow up!

Just then Nancy felt the bandanna around her wrists tear a little, allowing her hands to shift the slightest bit. Within moments, she pulled her hands free of the bandanna.

Yes!

Her hands flew to her ankles. In seconds they, too, were free. She yanked the bandanna from her mouth, trying to fight off the wooziness that threatened to overtake her at any second.

Coughing like crazy, she jumped toward Bess. It seemed like an eternity before she managed to untie first Bess and then Rhoda. As they stumbled coughing to the door, Nancy saw that the flames completely covered the three cans of turpentine.

"Quick!" she rasped.

The three of them ran out the door, gasping. They had gone only a few steps across the patio when the explosion came.

Boom!

The force shattered the glass in the French doors and sent Nancy, Bess, and Rhoda diving forward with their arms over their heads.

"That . . . was close!" Rhoda said, between gulping breaths.

As they pushed themselves to sitting, Shane appeared from around the side of the house. He ran toward them, his face tight with alarm. "What's happening?"

Nancy heard cries ring out from elsewhere in the house, as others realized something was wrong.

"Call the fire department and make sure there's no one in the house!" she cried, leaping to her feet. "We have to catch Gemma before she gets away."

"I can't believe this," Shane said, his eyes on the flames that burst out of Rhoda's office. "I was waiting by the fountain. It's been only a few minutes. I never dreamed . . ."

149

"No one blames you," Rhoda said. "We'd better split up and look for her. I'll cut off the exit to the road from the back lane."

Nancy grabbed Bess's arm and tugged her the other way, across the lawn. "Bess and I will cut through the woods this way to try to trap Gemma from the other side!"

"I'll call the fire department and check the house," Shane said.

The four of them ran off in three different directions. "I hope we're not too late," Bess said.

Nancy's lungs still burned from the smoke and turpentine fumes. Her eyes still stung, but as soon as she and Bess reached the front of the house, she made herself watch the woods carefully.

"What's happening?" Stu cried as he and a handful of other students came running up from the art studios. "What's all that smoke coming out of the house?"

"Have you seen Gemma Vance?" Bess asked. "It's important!"

He flicked a thumb toward the woods beyond the sculpture garden. "But—"

Nancy and Bess didn't wait to hear the rest. They raced toward the woods, leaving everyone gaping at the house with stunned expressions on their faces.

"Come on!" Nancy said.

They moved like lightning down the sloping lawn, then between two towering oaks as they entered the woods.

"I hear a car," Bess said as she and Nancy pounded over the leaves and branches that covered the hard-packed earth.

Nancy heard the engine, too. It chugged, then fell silent, and then chugged once more. "It sounds as if Gemma's motor isn't starting," she said. "We're in luck!"

Seconds later Nancy spotted a thick tangle of raspberry bushes. Gemma's blue car was parked just beyond them, in the rutted lane, and Gemma was behind the wheel. Her face was red with frustration as she yanked the key in the ignition to the right. Then she glanced up, and her eyes met Nancy's.

"It can't be," Nancy heard Gemma say.

At that moment Nancy saw Rhoda's green minivan driving toward Gemma on the dirt road.

"She's trapped!" Bess cried.

Seeing Rhoda, Gemma threw open the door of the sedan. She jumped out and began pushing past the raspberry bushes, yanking her clothes free of thorns as she went.

"No way. You're not going to get away this time," Nancy muttered. She closed the distance between them in six running strides and grabbed Gemma's arm just as she pulled free of the last raspberry branch.

"No!" Gemma tried to pull away, but Nancy lashed out with a kick that sent Gemma flying to the ground. Seconds later Nancy had Gemma's arms behind her back. Bess and Rhoda untied the bandannas that had been dangling around their necks, and Nancy used them to bind Gemma's hands together at the wrists.

"Give it up, Gemma," Nancy said. "It's over."

"Great speech, Dad," Nancy said to Carson Drew on Saturday night.

The banquet hall at the River Heights Plaza Hotel sparkled with light. Flashing cameras caught Carson in his tuxedo as he bent to give Nancy a kiss when he returned to their table from the podium. Applause rang out from the fifteen tables, and glasses clinked as they were raised in toast to Carson.

"Given the events of the past few days, I hardly feel *I'm* the person who should be honored here," he said, taking his seat next to Nancy. "The real heroes tonight are you three." He nodded at Nancy, Bess, and Rhoda.

Carson's secretary, Ms. Hanson, applauded along with the mayor and everyone else at the table. "Hear, hear!" said Ms. Hanson. "From what I've heard, you were very brave."

Nancy felt her face redden. It was embarrassing to be praised in public—especially with the mayor sitting at their table. "It wasn't such a big deal," she said.

"Oh, don't be so modest." Marianna Pennington spoke up from across the table, where she sat with

Bruce. "Thanks to you, Gemma Vance is behind bars, where she belongs."

"It's a shame we weren't able to stop her *before* she started the fire in my office," Rhoda said. "I'm afraid the whole back of the house will have to be re-built."

"Don't worry about that. I've already got a construction crew lined up," Bruce said.

Leaning close to Nancy, Bess whispered, "I guess Bruce wants everyone to know once and for all that he's not the bad guy we thought he was."

"He's not the only one we were wrong about," Nancy said. She paused as a waiter took the remains of her dessert, a creamy strawberry shortcake, from in front of her. "Now Shane can spend time with Rosie without having to worry about hiding his past from her or about defending himself from our accusations."

"Shane is a hero, too, for helping catch Gemma," Rhoda said. "I think getting to know Rosie has given Shane a reason to turn his life around."

Bess took a last bite of her shortcake before the waiter whisked her plate away, too. Shaking her head slowly, she said, "I still can't believe Gemma held such a grudge against you for all those years, Rhoda. It's creepy."

"It's a shame," Carson said. "I've spoken to the prosecutor handling her case, and he assures me Gemma will receive counseling while she's in jail.

With luck, she'll come to see that trying to burn up buildings and hurt people is no way to solve her problems."

"In the end her crimes were worse than anything she accused anyone else of. If she'd had her way . . ." Nancy said.

She didn't need to finish her sentence. Her father slipped an arm protectively around her shoulders and said, "She didn't, and all of you are safe, thank goodness."

"I wish I could say the same for the newspaper articles I promised you, Ms. Hanson," Nancy said. She glanced apologetically at her dad's secretary. "They all went up in smoke. Sorry."

"Newspaper articles?" Carson raised an inquiring eyebrow.

"Don't worry about it, Nancy," Ms. Hanson said. "I managed to get to the *News* office myself today, in time to put this together."

She reached under her chair for a leather-bound album with a ribbon tied around it. As she handed it to Carson, Bess turned to Nancy and laughed. "After what happened at River Arts," she said, "I'll bet there'll be a few newspaper headlines with *our* names in them."

Just then a photographer aimed his camera at their table and said, "Smile!"

"See?" Bess said, putting on her best smile as she leaned close to Nancy. "It's starting already!"